Dangerous Intentions

J. M. Robinson

Rockin' Robin Press, Nevada

Dangerous Intentions is a work of fiction.
Characters, names, incidents and places are products
of the author's imagination or they are used fictitiously. Any
resemblance to real persons living or dead is coincidental.

For my friend Terry Weldon
who is in a fight for life against an insidious disease.
Terry, you inspire women everywhere with your amazing
strength, courage, and endless joy.
With love, JMR

"I've learned from experience that the greater part of our
happiness or misery depends on our dispositions and not on
our circumstances."

Martha Washington

Chapter 1

Every morning, just like clockwork, the crusted dirt clod suddenly exploded into a wisp of alkali dust as he kicked it hard into the burned-out '57 Chevy. Before the fine white dust had a chance to settle, Chappy quickly spat on the rusted vehicle frame, grunting loudly as he did so. Not a day had gone by in forty years that he hadn't initiated this routine. He hated the rusty skeleton more than words could express and that overwhelming disgust provoked him with the same response each time he passed by its location on his daily journey across the property.

"Damn you to hell!" He snorted. The sight of the rusting hulk always filled his being with raging emotions until he was unable to contain his loathing and discontent. Somehow the mere act of spitting in disgust proved his only satisfactory release. Chappy Morgan, it seemed, was haunted by too many memories to count. The hulking piece of rusted metal essentially served as a beacon for the collection of ghosts that unavoidably invaded his solitary life.

Chapter 2

Morgan whistled for his dogs as they stopped to rummage through a scattering of sun bleached bones. Reluctantly he retraced his steps back over the fence stile in an effort to stop the dogs' scavenging adventure. He did not want the old remains to be scattered any distance beyond his own fence and he scolded the dogs again and again as they attempted to drag a large piece of cow hide under the five-wire barbed fence surrounding his property. With a loud grunt he hoisted the old hide and gave it his best toss. "Leave it be." he cautioned loudly as he stumbled slightly over a large clump of salt grass. The old man ascended the stile and stepped down the other side once again as he admonished his canine partners. "Don't borrow trouble, you two. Leave the ghosts to sleep in peace."

Chappy was tired. He couldn't remember a day when simple walking was more of a chore. His old legs had shuffled along the shoreline of Stillwater Point Reservoir so many times over the years that his path was as clearly marked as a cow trail through the soft mounds of salt grass and alkali dirt. Day after day he travelled the exact same route. He passed by the same bushes of rabbit brush, greasewood, and sage.

The same rotted out fence posts, the same old abandoned farm implements as well as the same tree stumps that had long since been washed ashore by the relentless wind across the water. Even the clusters of cattails and tule that grew along the ditch banks remained the same. Chappy's days were decorated with monotony. The land seemed to be caught in a time warp as if *Old Man Time* and *Mother Nature* literally stood still for the forty plus years old Mr. Morgan lived in the secluded and barren area.

But there had been changes, serious changes. And there were countless secrets in Chappy's life which would see the light of day if the old bleached bones on his property were disturbed or discovered. Some secrets were better left unknown. Besides, nothing good would come from waking the ghosts.

The one difference that a stranger might notice, however, was the addition of two stray dogs that joined him on his daily journey. Chappy couldn't recall how many different dogs there were over the years; but the most recent pair that followed him could be found every morning waiting patiently near the barbed wire fence surrounding his property. For some reason these two strays rarely ventured closer to his old cabin than that fence. It was as if the barbed barrier represented an unspoken rule and was not to be broken. Previous strays that he could remember came closer to his home and a couple of them had even lived under his porch for a few years.

Each of the current dogs seemed as tired and shaggy as Chappy himself as they followed closely behind him in silence. The larger of the two, a black lab with huge paws and sad dark eyes, was nearly always muddy or at least dusty from head to foot. He was accompanied by a smaller collie mix in perpetual need of brushing. The collie often had cockleburs and weeds tangled in his fine long hair and he walked with a noticeable limp on his right front leg. Chappy believed the dog had been caught in a trap at some time in its life which permanently damaged the collie's paw.

Casually the old codger named the two vagabond dogs just like he named the others over the years. He always used the same two names whether the dogs were male or female. The larger one he called *Joe* and the collie he named *Harry*. Strangely, the names always seemed to fit regardless of the breed of dog.

Even though the old man barely spoke above a whisper, the two canines happily responded to his voice with wagging tails and unwavering loyalty. Perhaps the dogs were curious about this old man who walked the same path to and from his home every day. Or maybe they were just lonesome for his deliberate and peaceful company. Whatever the reason, they often trailed along congenially as if to serve as his rear guard. Chappy always noticed when they were absent.

Over the years, Morgan came to know the Stillwater refuge like the back of his hand. A boat ramp and pit toilets were eventually built by wildlife officials and new culverts and flood gates were installed to better direct the water flows. Better roads were created and new rules and regulations were posted. But this modernization merely enticed more fishermen, hunters, and bird watchers to Chappy's private and isolated retreat. Yet his quest to view the thousands of shorebirds and water fowl that passed through the refuge on their migratory routes never wavered regardless of the strangers in attendance or the foul weather he encountered. He simply ignored all of it, except of course, for his two canine friends.

It could be said that Chappy Morgan was a man trapped in the wrong century. He made no excuses for his behavior – he just didn't want to have anyone around at any time for any reason. He did not need conversation or communion; in fact he wanted no human interaction whatsoever.

He might have been better suited to live among the early pioneers of Nevada when the historical town site of Stillwater was first founded in 1862 by the very small and sturdy population of farmers and cattle ranchers who ventured out West. During those days, the entire population of Churchill

County, Nevada was only 873 inhabitants for its 5,023 square miles of land. It was desolate indeed. In fact, had it not been for the resilient folks who were the earliest Nevada settlers, the Nevada State Legislature might have actually eliminated the entire county comprised of so few cattle ranchers, farmers, and businessmen. Luckily in 1875, eleven years after Nevada became the 35th state in 1864, a strong and independent Nevada politician by the name of Lemuel Allen was able to convince the standing Governor, Lewis R. Bradley to veto just such a bill and thus saved Churchill County from its premature demise.

The unregulated and meandering Carson River terminated in the nearby Stillwater marshes before the construction of the Lahontan Dam and reservoir in 1915. There was excellent hunting and fishing during the good water years before the river was tamed and it would have been much easier for Chappy to live off the land in those days. During drought years, though, the marshes were degraded with unusable stagnant salt water and thick alkali mud. And it was for that primary reason that the wildlife management area was established in 1949 during the presidency of Harry S. Truman. As a major fly-way for the same millions of migratory birds that Chappy loved and studied, legislation was enacted to supply fresh water to the 77,000 acre Stillwater National Wildlife Refuge to stave off summer droughts. It was a *catch-twenty-two* situation for the old man. More progress and better maintenance of the area was better for his beloved birds. But it also meant more visitors and more interruptions to his solitude.

Chappy grunted noisily as he set down the small easel, notebooks, and the box of charcoal pencils he brought with him to sketch the day's avian visitors. Although his breathing was quite labored, he stretched and yawned in the cool spring air as he gazed around at his beloved wildlife refuge. Still feeling stiff and short of breath, he found it an unusually difficult chore to lower his tired body down onto his favorite rock. He grumbled loudly once again as he dropped down the last few inches to the flat granite surface. His faithful traveling partners lay nearby with tails wagging as he finally lifted the brown sack lunch from his coat pocket. Neither dog made a move toward him but waited patiently for a simple shared crust of bread. Chappy tossed the familiar treat to each dog and poured a cup of strong black coffee from the small thermos he always carried. Refreshed with nourishment, he washed down the last of his sandwich and popped several ginger snap cookies into his mouth. Last, but not least, he threw a ginger snap to each of his grateful traveling companions. The breeze across the large pond was brisk and Chappy sensed that it was going to be a spectacular day for bird watching.

Chapter 3

Charles Preston Morgan was born in 1919, the only surviving child of Lester and Mary Morgan of Boston, Massachusetts. His frail and sickly mother was stricken by the terrible influenza epidemic in 1918, the year before his birth. She had barely survived the dreadful illness and loss of her third unborn child, a tiny baby girl.

Charles' father, the senior mister Morgan, was a wildly successful ship builder with a large fleet of his own vessels who made his fortune during World War I shipping materials and equipment for the U.S. Government. As such he was rarely at home with his family. In his place, Mary Morgan's mother, Ivy Johannson came to live in their Boston home to assist her daughter with the couples' newborn son.

From his birth, Grandmother Ivy fondly referred to the towheaded boy as Chappy. The nickname stuck with him long after his loving grandmother passed away. *Chappy* became the name that young Charles Morgan cherished.

Chappy's father, Lester Morgan, was a hulk of a man with a booming deep voice and unruly dark red hair and beard. He had a pension for bar maids and was considered by most God-fearing folks to be a complete scallywag.

His successful businesses allowed him countless opportunities to taste the female form in many exotic cities around the world. Unfortunately this extended travel left his family at home in Boston virtually forgotten. Sadly, young Chappy Morgan grew up with only the guidance and love of his elderly grandmother, pale sickly mother, and a variety of servants.

Charles grew to manhood in his father's absence as his ailing mother continued to suffer poor health. She was confined to a sanitarium with constant care just before Chappy left for his advanced studies in California at Stanford University in 1939. The handsome and dashing Charles Preston Morgan was destined for something different, something unknown, something wonderful. And he wanted to be as far away from Boston as possible.

Chapter 4

Warm and sunny Palo Alto, California agreed with Chappy Morgan from the moment he arrived at the train station. He gladly traded his east coast woolens for cool linen and cotton. The weather was a wonderful change for him and the informal university setting was very appealing to the tall good-looking young man from the East.

Unlike the sophisticated beachgoers of the Atlantic coastline, the relaxed style of Pacific sunbathers offered him abundant opportunities to meet the beautiful coeds who sought sunshine and relaxation from their daily grind and pursuit of academia. With his wallet stuffed full of money and boasting an extraordinary sense of self- confidence, Chappy Morgan quickly left his personal mark on the college dating scene. He cut a very wide swath through the available single women he happily encountered near the sparkling waters and sandy white beaches of the California coast.

After the outbreak of World War II, Stanford University, like many other universities across the nation, was committed to improving its military defense education and general technical training.

As a result of the surprise attack on Pearl Harbor by the Japanese in 1941, the entire university system benefited from increased government spending and war related contracts. The busy university stepped to the forefront of research facilities where electrical engineering became a primary focus of its curriculum and the main focus of young handsome Charles Morgan as well.

Chappy was a mature and incredibly intelligent twenty-year-old which made it very easy for him to excel in the university setting. His first two years of classes were merely child's play. But things changed dramatically for him in 1942 when his mother, who was essentially alone in Boston, passed away in the Massachusetts sanitarium. Chappy did not return to Boston upon her death nor did he ever visit his former home again. His arrogant father chose not to honor his deceased wife with a funeral service which devastated young Charles.

This neglect, along with his own sense of guilt and grief, shook him to his very core. It prompted him to burn all bridges with his former life in Boston. And, of course, that decision primarily targeted his father Lester. Charles Morgan simply closed the book on that chapter of his life and never .looked back again. Some might even go so far as to say he became somewhat of a broken man. As a result of his mother's death, Charles became an intensely serious student. He literally studied nonstop around the clock until he acquired advanced degrees in both mechanical and electrical engineering. He later continued with his dedicated research until his Doctorate of Aeronautical Engineering was completed.

Charles was driven to achieve greatness forsaking his personal life in the process. His playboy attitudes and behaviors of the past were long forgotten as he became an engineering phenomenon. He soon accepted a teaching position as a fully accredited professor and eventually became Dean of the Engineering Department all while he continued with his advanced research in the field of aviation.

Chapter 5

After twenty years, first as a student and then as an educator, Charles Morgan left the world of academia for a life as an aeronautical research guru in private industry. He designed top secret technologies that the aviation giants, like Boeing, Douglas, and the National Aeronautical Space Administration (NASA) were interested in and were willing to pay top dollar to acquire. Chappy was surrounded by lawyers, public relation firms, and accountants for the first time in his life and it seemed tedious and foreign to him. His life was dedicated to the pursuit of scientific study and research. All the rest was an insignificant bother to him like that of a pesky mosquito.

Still a bachelor in 1959, with no desire to be otherwise, dashing forty-year-old Charles Morgan dutifully, and all but begrudgingly, accepted an invitation to a cocktail party given in his honor by Fredrick Winston. Winston was an aggressive investment banker who was in hard pursuit of a financial partnership with Chappy's elite company. The brilliant man detested such affairs, but Fredrick Winston was a persuasive player in the San Francisco financial district. As a matter of course, Chappy's personal attorney, Simon Pearle encouraged

Professor Morgan to be more accessible to the important people of the city. And because Simon spoke with a heavy French accent, his very presence added a soothing dimension to Chappy's life. Therefore, the suave attorney continually persuaded him to do things he would have normally avoided.

Charles Morgan was an incredibly wealthy man in his own right due in part to his perpetually frugal lifestyle, and mostly because he inherited a substantial fortune from the family owned shipping business after the death of his father. But he did not relish that fact nor display it in any public means other than his significant endowments to the ballet and philharmonic orchestra.

Chappy's fondness for the arts came from the early childhood stories his Grandmother Ivy told him about the days when his own mother, Mary Johannson-Morgan had been a beautiful and promising ballerina back in Boston. That was, of course, before she met and married his father and traded her hopes and dreams of life on stage with the Royal Ballet for a life of ill-health, shame, and loneliness at the hands of the arrogant and adulterous Lester Morgan.

As Chappy readied himself for his appearance at Winston's cocktail party, he stepped onto his balcony to enjoy another beautiful California sunset. He had grown fond of the view from his stately old house overlooking the San Francisco Bay and the Golden Gate Bridge. It was always a breathtaking sight from the hill as the west coast colors of sunset gradually changed from hues of soft pink and orange into deep reds and purples.

He loved the view of sailboats moving crisply across the bay around Alcatraz and Angel Islands. And he often felt himself mesmerized by the car lights twinkling in the distance as they made their way across the elegant bay bridge as nightfall came to the city.

It always brought Chappy Morgan great peace and comfort to know that he was a long, long way from the Commonwealth of Massachusetts.

Chapter 6

One simple thing that the brilliant Dr. Charles Morgan had not done in the last decade was to drive his own car. Driving seemed a mundane and irritating task for him as the California traffic continued to expand. He plainly found it a better use of his time to let his driver, Lionel Carver fight through the traffic jams and highway construction projects that littered the main thoroughfares.

Charles was better served to read the latest myriad of books and journals he selected for himself and to write his detailed and lengthy critiques of them rather than fuss with basic transportation needs.

Lionel was ready and waiting with the shiny black 1959 Rolls Royce Silver Wraith as Chappy exited the house and thanked him kindly for his prompt service. Lionel was a connoisseur of cars and a very good friend. Chappy had given the war veteran free reign as to the make and model of car he preferred to drive as money was certainly not the issue. The Silver Wraith was an amazing automobile and Chappy was pleased with Lionel's fine new selection.

The Silver Wraith approached Nob Hill and the historic hotel where Fredrick Winston waited. He would be terribly impatient no doubt. Chappy groaned at the prospect of spending the next few hours locked in glib conversation with a man he despised. It was torturous for him to attend such functions regardless of the circumstances. But luckily the views of San Francisco from the luxurious and world renowned hotel were magnificent. With the panoramic view of the city lights and the bay at night Chappy would be able to see Union Square, the financial district, and Fisherman's wharf. He was becoming familiar with each location as a recent newcomer to the city

Fredrick Winston, an extremely rotund and very short man by most standards, stood only five-foot-five-inches tall. But his pompous and snobbish attitudes bore the signs of a real giant. He was rude and arrogant with an inappropriate sense of humor which Chappy found particularly distasteful and regrettable.

If truth be known, there was a hint of Lester Morgan in the short man's behavior which always struck a sour note for the successful entrepreneur. It would require Chappy's last ounce of strength and patience to merely tolerate the banker who so keenly wanted a piece of his research company. Winston was also an extraordinarily wealthy and powerful man which was rather deceptive to an outsider at first glance of his messy unkempt appearance. He nearly always wore several days' growth of grey stubble across his face which accentuated his bulbous and purple alcoholic nose. His refusal to wear starched shirts and collars along with a suit coat in serious need of pressing always left him looking rumpled and undone. Winston continually refused to have his shoes polished and shined which detract greatly from the image one might expect of a successful businessman and multi-millionaire. In short, he very often looked like an unmade bed. Tonight would be no exception to that rule.

Fredrick Winston's tremendous fortune was won by bold and devious financial dealings.

These primarily resulted from his very close association with the United States Government after the end of World War II. He was reportedly a childhood acquaintance of President Dwight D. Eisenhower and as such he surreptitiously garnered extensive access to and benefit from each branch of Congress along with countless other governmental and military agencies.

Winston also inherited a vast fortune from his late father who had been a successful railroad magnate. He was the type one could read about in history books regarding the settlement of the wild American West. He, too, was a ruthless man who lived a very rough and rugged life. He was known to be a heartless individual who supposedly stole whatever couldn't be legitimately purchased.

The rotund Fredrick's late wife, Anna Winston was also the only heir to an astounding fortune. Her father and grandfather had been notorious diamond merchants known throughout Asia, South America, and Europe.

History has shown that it was a common practice in elite society for someone in a position of power and wealth to marry another with even greater wealth. This was certainly true in Winston's case. Money may have oozed from his very pores, but Chappy believed Fredrick Winston to be a despicable and desperate character. He wanted nothing to do with the inconsiderate and callous man.

The rumor was that Fredrick liked things more than a bit rough with his women, of whom there were purportedly many before and after his wife's death from emphysema. Chappy intensely disliked the man without really knowing him simply because he was thought to be an abusive cad. That type of behavior was completely intolerable and unacceptable to the successful Charles P. Morgan, PhD.

Simply said, Fredrick Winston's revolting attitudes and boorish behavior far exceeded the boundaries Chappy accepted from anyone in his own life. Winston's annoying voice and image brought unwanted memories of Boston flooding back into Dr. Morgan's life from the darkest recesses of his mind.

Chapter 7

"Here's the man of the hour now!" the short man yelled brashly as Chappy and Simon entered the elegant suite. The professor's cobalt blue eyes burned a hole through his host.

Immediately after the smooth and eloquent French attorney's introductions had been made, the tall blond replied void of all emotion, "How do you do?"

"Belly up to the bar, Morgan, and don't be shy. Supply is endless around here," the short man said slapping Charles on the back. "With a brain like yours you can risk losing a few fucking brain cells on this expensive imported champagne I've arranged for you to drink. This shit cost me five-hundred-dollars a bottle and it still tastes like piss!"

Chappy accepted a crystal glass of champagne from an exotically beautiful black waitress as his host continued with a derogatory remark concerning the young woman's large firm breasts. The drunken Winston fiddled with the sash of her crisp white apron. After a quick slap to her buttocks, the insufferable short man added rudely, "Morgan, I say if a man's not thinking about pussy then he's damn well not worth a fuck." Winston was already disgustingly loud as Chappy walked away to speak privately with Simon about terminating the meeting early.

"Just where in the hell do you think you're going, Morgan, I'm not finished with you yet," Fredrick bellowed, angry that the brilliant engineer had turned his back on him. "We have business to discuss and you can ill-afford to piss me off tonight. I can squash you like a stinking little maggot with the snap of my fingers."

As the fat man snapped his fingers, Charles stopped dead still in his tracks not certain of his own intentions. As he slowly turned around to confront his belligerent and drunken host, flashes of his father shot through his mind again. Hatred and anger roiled inside him.

Meanwhile, Chappy's attorney Simon Pearle immediately stepped between the two men to diplomatically resolve the issue before it boiled over into an embarrassing public display. Many of San Francisco's premier businessmen and civic leaders were present in the room and Simon knew it was prudent of him to protect Chappy's interest even if the brilliant man himself did not think so.

"No need for anger, Monsieur Fredrick," Simon insisted quietly as he led Winston toward the large windows overlooking the city. "We're all friends here tonight and Dr. Morgan is waiting to hear some more about your interest in his aviation research. We need to be clear headed to understand the details. So come, Monsieur, please sit down right here by this magnificent view of the sea, quelle belle vue de la mer, and talk to us about your ideas. Oui, oui, sit down right here Monsieur Fredrick s'il vous plait."

"Bring me a double whiskey straight up little darlin' and keep them coming," the swaggering man demanded of the nervous and humiliated waitress as he slapped her curvaceous buttocks once again. The despicable character rejoiced in his insult of the lovely young woman and recognized immediately that he had pushed her beyond the point of tears. Victory was his in no small measure as he smiled broadly.

Winston let Simon select an over-stuffed chair for him nearest the grand piano in the corner of the room. The pianist was playing a soothing arrangement of *Clair de lune*, by Claude Debussy. Simon mistakenly believed the relaxing music would help calm their agitated host, but that simple thought soon proved to be an error in judgment. After quickly surveying the room to count the eyes upon him, Fredrick deliberately continued with another loud outburst. "Don't touch me, Frenchie, gawdammit, I'm warning you for the last time! I don't like being coddled. Don't try to handle me like a fuckin' cripple."

Charles hesitated and then followed Simon's lead as he sat opposite Winston where he could look out at the city lights and still keep the banker in view. Simon sat between the two men with the window at his back.

After Fredrick Winston downed his whiskey he wiped his mouth on the cuff of his white dress shirt. With continuing arrogance, he and the French attorney briefly discussed a business proposition regarding Chappy's company while the blond engineer sat by stoically and gazed at the city lights.

Winston's words became increasingly vulgar and Charles instinctively knew there was no way he was going to become involved with such a revolting human being. Nothing the smooth talking and suave Simon Pearle could say would change his mind. Simon, at the same time, also realized by the professor's total silence that Chappy was not at all interested in Winston's deal. He knew that it was time for the distinguished blond man to make a speedy exit with the least possible complication.

"Monsieur Fredrick, if you would be so kind as to send your papers to my office I will review them and discuss them with Doctor Morgan. We will be happy to consider your offer. Thank you for your kind hospitality but we must be going. Thank you, merci, thank you very much, merci beaucoup."

"Well, I'll be go to hell! Can't this fancy-ass Doctor speak for himself?" Winston demanded. "You think you're too good for me don't you, Charley boy. Well I have never been so gawdamned insulted in my life as to have a show-off scientist snub me like this." Turning with a dramatic wave toward the people in the room he asked, "Just who in the hell does he think he is? I bent over backwards to impress this son-of-a-bitch tonight and now he thinks he's too damn good to talk to me."

Fredrick Winston slurred his words, flailed his arms, knocked over a table lamp, and sent brass and shattering glass crashing to the floor. He created a deliberate commotion which drew the attention of everyone in the room. During his tirade, a big wad of his spittle landed on the French attorney's cheek and slowly dripped down onto Simon's lapel. A collective gasp rippled through the hushed crowd. As Simon stepped away from the irate drunken banker, he calmly wiped off the white glob of thick mucus with his monogrammed silk handkerchief.

"Please, Monsieur Fredrick, send your papers to my office, s;il vous plait," the gentle lawyer pleaded. "I will take care of the rest. Bonsoir, Monsieur Winston, we must be going, I bid you adieu."

As Chappy stood to dismiss himself, the old banker took a swipe at him with an outstretched palm, but the tall blond easily dodged the drunken blow. With hatred in his eyes Chappy responded calmly to the angry but tragic figure staggering uneasily in front of him.

"I am Doctor Charles Preston Morgan, Sir, and I'll thank you kindly to treat my attorney and good friend, Mr. Simon Pearle with the respect and dignity he rightly deserves." Laughing, Chappy placed his hands on his hips and then continued. "But as I say that, Mr. Winston, I am reminded that any gesture of appropriate respect or dignity Simon might deserve is far and above what you are capable of giving him."

Charles paused a moment to collect his thoughts and then continued speaking as he boldly wagged his index finger at his host. "Furthermore, I am advising you, Mr. Winston, to never speak to me again. Not in public or in private. I have the God-given right, as do we all, Sir, to refuse to speak to whomever I choose be he drunk or sober, educated or idiot. And you fit smack dab in the middle of both. Don't bother sending your papers to Mr. Pearle as I have no intention of doing any sort of business with you now or at any time in the future. You, Mr. Winston, are a sorry excuse for a man. I would risk being bankrupt and destitute rather than to ever be involved with the likes of you. You are a pathetic bully and a waste of my precious time. Perhaps you might consider calling on your old friend, Howard Hughes about your sudden interest in aviation. I hear he has a lot going on these days and the two of you might well strike a mutual agreement. Good night, Sir. I can see myself out. Let's go Simon; I've had enough of this vulgarity."

Slightly embarrassed by the entire scene, the French attorney added calmly, "Au revoir, Monsieur Fredrick. Au revoir. Merci beaucoup."

Chapter 8

Chappy was reading the morning *Chronicle* and chuckling at the society columnist's account of his less than ideal incident with Fredrick Winston when his long time housekeeper, Laurel Saint James announced the French attorney's arrival.

"Good morning, Sir, would you care for a cup of tea or coffee?" Laurel asked as she greeted Simon Pearle.

"Bonjour, Madame Laurel, beautiful day is it not?" Simon asked. "A coffee would be lovely, merci."

"Bonjour, Monsieur Charles, I see you have found the society column this morning. From the sound of it you kicked at the devil himself, le Diable."

As he put the newspaper down, Chappy laughed and said, "Don't give it another thought Simon. There's nothing that old fool can do that I would give two cents for. He's wrong if he thinks I give a tinker's damn about what he says to the newspaper's reporter.

It's my company he wants and my contracts too, and I swear on my poor dead mother's soul that he will never be my partner as long as I am still breathing. Never!"

"Merci beaucoup, Madame, this is wonderful". Simon stated politely in between sips of hot steaming coffee.

"You should send the cranky old bastard your dry cleaning bill, Simon. That would serve him right for spitting on you like he did." Charles added with animation. "What a pompous ass he was last night, puffed up like a proverbial peacock. I must say you handled yourself extremely well old boy. You deserve a gold star for behavior like that. I think you're much too polite for your own good. Any other foolish sod might have spat back at Winston and created a giant ruckus in that elegant suite overlooking the skyline. He certainly deserved to be taken down a notch or two and I should have done that for myself."

Simon quickly responded, "No, no, no, Monsieur, tis better to let, how do you say, sleeping dogs lie."

As Charles leaned back in his recliner he lamented, "Well, Simon, I can say with confidence that Fredrick Winston is like most of the bullies I've known. He's a big blow-hard who actually has very little between his ears. He rules by intimidation and I've known men like him all my life. We'll all be better off if we just give him a wide berth and forget he's even around."

Simon shook his head in disagreement. A few seconds later he reconsidered and added, "Oui, Monsieur, that maybe so, but I fear he is the devil himself. Le Diable. No good will come from him as long as his shadow is upon the earth. Oui, oui, le Diable!" A few minutes later Simon continued. "Charles, I brought some proposals for you to review if you please, s'il vous plait. It is regarding NASA and their future Explorer and Apollo space programs along with several offers from the other agencies we spoke about. Take your time reading them as they are very detailed and complicated. I do not want any misunderstandings with them in the future."

"Okay, Simon," Charles stated.

"I'll do my best to read these as soon as I can and thank you again for your personal assistance and friendship. I mean it Simon. You're a fine man and you have always been a very good friend."

"Merci, Charles, I must go. I will let myself out. Au revoir, Adieu, and have a nice day." Laughing he added, "And what is it you say here in America, ah yes, *the bill is in the mail!* Au revoir, Madame Laurel, merci beaucoup. Thank you for the wonderful coffee," Simon sang as he tipped his hat to his friends and hurried toward the door.

"Good bye, my friend, the same to you," Charles added confidently. "I'll bring these back to your office as soon as I can Simon, but it may be a few days. I have several important tests pending at the laboratory."

Chapter 9

The Silver Wraith was stopped in traffic with Chappy deep in concentration over one of his journals when Lionel turned up the radio to hear the details of a recent plane crash. "Who's the newscaster talking about, Lionel? Do you know anything about it?" Chappy inquired, suddenly distracted from his reading.

"Yes, Sir, it's a sad day, Mr. Charles," Lionel responded. "A mighty sad day. That plane crash snuffed out the lives of four good men who were some mighty fine musicians. The pilot was killed along with Buddy Holly, Ritchie Valens, and the Big Bopper himself, Jiles Perry Richardson, Jr. They were in Iowa somewhere and their plane crashed in the fog. All four men died. Yes, Sir it's a sad, sad day for music lovers all over the world."

"Do you know their music well, Lionel?" Charles asked with curiosity.

"Oh, yes, Sir, I just love their music." Lionel responded as he turned up the radio. "Listen to this one now, Mr. Charles. The dj's playing one of the really good songs."

"It's Buddy Holly's *Peggy Sue*. That's a good one for sure; one of the best I think. What do you think, Mr. Charles? Do you like it?"

Dangerous Intentions

"Yes, Lionel, I must agree it's a pretty catchy tune." Charles, a bit embarrassed by his fundamental lack of musical knowledge continued. "I'm sorry I've never paid much attention to popular music before. I didn't know anything about these men. You'll have to introduce me to some of your other favorites when you have the time."

"Yes Sir, Mr. Charles, I'd be happy to," Lionel added with pleasure as he watched his employer in the rearview mirror. "Music is good for your soul. It lifts the burdens right off a tired man's back. Yes indeedy it surely does."

As the traffic began to move slowly away from the stop light, Chappy's attention was drawn to a beautiful woman in a new red and white Corvette with the convertible top down. She was traveling in the lane next to the Rolls Royce. The music of Peggy Sue was blaring on her car radio as the young woman sang the lyrics at the top of her voice and kept time on the steering wheel with her dazzling red painted fingernails. Her long dark mane of hair was swept back with a beautiful silk scarf tied loosely around her face which perfectly framed her delicate features. Each time she smiled with the music she displayed sparkling white teeth, the brightest and whitest most perfect teeth that Chappy had ever seen. She had a gorgeous smile and rosy cheeks and he simply could not stop watching her.

"Now there's someone who appreciates good music," Lionel said laughing out loud. "You got to feel the music, Mr. Charles, feel it right down to your toes."

"I can see that, Lionel," Chappy added, mesmerized by the view. "She's lovely, just lovely. And she's certainly feeling something special alright. Let's follow her!"

Lionel Carver was flabbergasted at the request. Such a thing had never been asked of him in all the years he had been Charles Morgan's driver. As the '60 Corvette sped away from the stoplight, Lionel was thrilled to do the same. "Yes Sir, Mr.

Charles, we can certainly do that," he responded with a gleeful smile and a heavy foot.

The Corvette moved smartly through the traffic in the financial district as Lionel struggled to keep up. At one point he thought he'd lost the sports car when it suddenly ducked behind a large delivery van but it abruptly reappeared and both cars were caught side-by-side together again at another red light.

The beautiful woman was still singing as Ritchie Valen's *La Bamba* blared on the car radio. Chappy felt an instant connection to the stunning stranger because the same music played simultaneously inside the Silver Wraith as he watched her swing and sway with the music. She was totally uninhibited as her beautiful body danced to the music inside of her red and white convertible.

Her alluring long red fingernails kept perfect rhythm on the steering wheel enticing Chappy to duplicate their rhythm by tapping his own fingers on the window sill of the Rolls Royce. He was intoxicated by the vision.

All of the windows of the chauffeured vehicle were rolled down allowing the music from both car radios to completely fill the air surrounding the immediate area of the stoplight. The drums and bass vibrated the Rolls Royce in an impromptu tribute to the departed musician and both Chappy and Lionel enjoyed the stimulating effect as they waited in the warm sunshine for the green light.

Just as the music stopped, the light turned green. The dark-haired beauty in the new sports car lingered for a long moment.

As she stared at the men in the shiny black Rolls Royce, she smiled quite modestly at Lionel and then with flirtatious animation at Chappy in the back seat. With excitement she yelled "nice car" before she sped off in the direction of the Golden Gate Bridge amid honking horns from the irritated drivers behind her.

Dangerous Intentions

The dark-haired stranger was totally out of sight in a few seconds. Chappy's heart sank at the prospect of her getting away without a proper introduction. His pulse pounded in his head as he clenched his fist and pressed it into the palm of his other hand over and over again. His breathing quickened. He simply had not felt this alive in years and she was getting away!

As the Silver Wraith rounded the next corner, the very same hand-painted long silk scarf she had been wearing miraculously floated across the air in front of them and landed gracefully on a blooming red rose bush on the opposite side of the boulevard. Without hesitation Lionel pulled the vehicle to the side of the street and brought the shiny black car to an abrupt halt. He clamored out of the Silver Wraith and carefully avoided the heavy oncoming traffic as he snatched up the silk scarf, ran back across the street, and slid back behind the wheel with an appreciative Chappy Morgan in the back seat.

"Good thinking, old man, good thinking indeed!" Chappy bellowed as the chauffeur tossed the elegant scarf into the back seat and drove on down the street. With the sudden release of emotions too long contained, Charles Morgan pressed the silk scarf to his nose for a few seconds and inhaled the magnificent scent of its beautiful owner deep into his being. He simply allowed the sweet fragrance of her perfume to permeate his soul and stimulate his senses as he became lost in his own wondrous thoughts.

Suddenly inspired he added, "Let's get a drink somewhere and celebrate, Lionel. I can't tell you when I've had this much fun."

Chapter 10

Several days later, Charles Morgan was still consumed with thoughts of the beautiful woman in the red and white convertible. Every day he and Lionel drove the exact same route in anticipation of seeing her again with hopes for a chance encounter and the opportunity to return the elegant hand-painted silk scarf she had lost. The brilliant man was totally distracted from his work to the point of obsession. He was completely unprepared for such an emotional attachment to a perfect stranger and was caught off balance by the entire situation. Charles Morgan was out of his element like a fish out of water.

On the thirteenth evening of their trips around the city in search of the Corvette, Lionel was in a particularly jovial mood. He and Chappy had developed a much deeper bond of friendship with their daily escapades in search of the mysterious woman and he was thoroughly enjoying this special time with his employer.

As he whistled quietly to the tune of Peggy Sue and cornered the Rolls Royce onto California Avenue, he suddenly let out a long wolf whistle which alerted Chappy in the back seat. The illusive dark-haired feminine figure was climbing out of the red and white Corvette less than a block ahead of them.

Dangerous Intentions

"Do I pull in, Mr. Charles or drive on by?" he asked with a sudden sense of excitement.

"Pull in, Lionel, by all means. Pull in and park right next to her!" Charles responded anxiously. "Good eye, my man, good eye. If you'll be so kind as to wait right here I should only be a few minutes. I'll just run inside the restaurant and return her scarf."

"Take your time, Mr. Charles. Take your time." Lionel said calmly with a wide-eyed grin. "I've got all the time in the world for this beautiful lady. I'll just grab a cup of coffee and sit right here till you're ready to go."

Chapter 11

Charles Morgan fell in love with Caroline Righetti from the moment he first spoke to her. He fell hard, fast, and without a second thought. Her voice was soft and soothing and Chappy was mesmerized by the sound of her. She was wonderfully smart and equally beautiful and her sense of humor was totally beguiling.

In their first year together Chappy found a new zest for life. Caroline's enthusiasm was contagious and the usually stoic professor gradually came back to life in her presence. She was utterly and deliciously charming and he simply could not resist the new emotions, new desires, and new hopes for the future that she awakened in him. Chappy's attitudes and interests changed along with his wardrobe and sense of style. Suddenly he stood taller, felt stronger, and looked even more handsome than ever before. Caroline Righetti was the reason why. Thirty year old Caroline Righetti, M.D. had just completed her medical residency at San Francisco's Mount Zion Hospital in the specialty field of cardiology.

She had been drawn to medicine after the death of her mother years earlier. As an only child, Caroline had been terribly spoiled by her adoring mother and over indulgent father. Ignoring her scruples, she became a wild and reckless youth as she traveled the world with her rich friends from similar family situations. There had been no rules and certainly no consequences in the luxurious life of the spoiled little rich girl as she made her way across the continents and especially into Italy, France and Monaco. She was drawn to the vulgar playgrounds of the world's rich where strangers spent their money foolishly and their time in misdirected abandon. Her world turned up-side-down, however, with the death of her young mother while Caroline was away in Europe.

Her bubble burst with that one swift moment in time and she was forever changed. She was totally devastated and yet miraculously saved at the same time. Ultimately she dedicated her life to helping others and became a brilliant and compassionate cardiac surgeon.

Caroline was a striking beauty with long dark hair and sympathetic brown eyes. Her skin was like delicate white porcelain throughout her tall thin body and she moved with the grace of a ballerina. She had a European look about her which intrigued Chappy although she spoke little of her background and even less of her parents. Some things were kept very private by Dr. Righetti just as they were with Dr. Morgan. For that reason and many others, the handsome couple was a perfect match. Their romance bloomed slowly at first as the shy and cautious professor and Caroline were both deeply-rooted in their chosen careers. But then by 1961 the professor threw caution to the wind and Caroline moved into his home overlooking the San Francisco Bay. Chappy simply adored her. He was the happiest with Caroline that he had ever been in his life. They were a very compatible, peaceful, and loving couple as each one complimented the other.

Both young lovers continued to study and mature in their chosen fields. They became two halves of the whole and although marriage was never discussed they knew they would be together for a life time.

Chapter 12

After the inauguration of John Fitzgerald Kennedy as the 35th President of the United States, military contracts once again changed substantially in the fields of aviation and space exploration. Chappy's company was on the forefront of both technologies and business was booming.

Periodically, Fredrick Winston would rear his ugly head and connive to force his way into Chappy's research firm. There were several near misses for the elite company but the clever Simon Pearle always prevailed on Doctor Morgan's behalf and kept the belligerent man at bay. Winston proved to be a very hostile and voracious shark in the competitive waters of the business world. It soon became Simon's primary mission to protect Charles Morgan from being eaten alive.

Winston, it seemed, was always simmering somewhere in the background, eager to interrupt Chappy's life at any opportunity. But the determined scientist provided a keen challenge for Fredrick Winston. Although Dr. Morgan was an involuntary target, he also became a very formidable opponent.

For some reason the two men had taken an instant dislike to one another and Chappy's solution was to simply give the horrible Fredrick Winston a wide berth and pretend that the bully did not exist. Right or wrong it was his personal choice.

Dangerous Intentions

Winston's choice, on the other hand, was to provide as much turmoil and interference to Dr. Morgan and his elite company as was humanly possible. He did it out of pure greed and a misdirected sense of personal delight.

By the summer of 1961, the Mercury space program was in full swing. Chappy was required to do a lot of traveling to the south coast of Florida which meant leaving Caroline alone in San Francisco to practice medicine. When American Gus Grissom was launched into sub-orbital space flight by the United States, he was their second astronaut to be launched into the great unknown. Grissom was the pilot of the Mercury-Redstone 4 capsule aptly named the Liberty Bell 7. The launch was a huge success, but Chappy's company suffered a tremendous blow when the Liberty Bell 7 sank immediately after splashdown due to the premature opening of the capsule's hatch. The hatch failure caused a total loss of the company's expected technological results which set his research and design team several months behind schedule.

As rumblings of another war began to circulate throughout the industry, Chappy had wisely taken his company into yet another direction for research and development. Helicopters were to be in the forefront of the suspected war efforts and by December of 1961, Vertol H-21C Shawnee helicopters were sent by air craft carrier to South Viet Nam. The unpopular war was yet another political hot potato for the United States but it meant extraordinarily busy times and huge paychecks for Chappy and his thriving company.

At the same time, just a few miles away, Doctor Caroline Righetti was incredibly busy at Mount Zion Hospital where the experimental pace maker was being tested on her critically ill cardiac patients.

The new technology proved to be a promising medical breakthrough and the beautiful doctor Righetti was proud to be associated with the hospital's teaching facility.

In the infant stages of their early design, the pacemakers were quite large and cumbersome. From the beginning, however, they were extending the lives of many of her critically ill patients all around the globe. She was pleased to have such a profound and positive influence on people's lives. Privately Caroline knew that she owed her brilliant success to her loving mother Anna.

Chapter 13

In February of 1963, Caroline and Chappy held their third *silk scarf celebration*, a tradition they began after 1960 to honor the day they met. Each year they invited their closest friends, including Lionel Carver and his new bride Laurel Saint James to an elegant evening at the hotel located at Number One Nob Hill. Caroline especially loved The Room of The Dons with its beautiful and colorful seven-foot-high panels painted by Frank Von Sloun and Maynard Dixon in 1926 for the hotel's grand re-opening.

The room was large, yet maintained an intimate appeal which suited their gathering nicely on such a happy occasion. The table settings were stylish, the food delicious, and the service impeccable.

Chappy arranged for a six piece ensemble of musicians to provide the music for his guests' dancing pleasure throughout the evening and also to perform a special rendition of the legendary Buddy Holly's Peggy Sue. The famous lyrics and tune had become the couples' favorite song and brought tears of laughter each year as they shared the story of their first encounter. But the highlight of the celebration was always Chappy's gift of a beautiful hand-painted silk scarf for each woman in the room and Caroline's red rose boutonniere for every gentleman.

"May each one of you, our dear friends, fall in love again tonight during this wonderful evening of happy celebration. May the soft breezes blow gently at your back and keep your silk scarves forever floating in the air. God bless you all."

"Here. Here. To Caroline and Charles."

Chapter 14

As Chappy and Caroline bid farewell to their last guests, Simon Pearle rushed out of the hotel elevator in a most agitated state.

"Pardon moi, Monsieur Charles, le Diable is headed this way on the next elevator. Perhaps you and Dr. Righetti should take the stairs immediately if you please, s'il vous plait, and thus avoid a most untimely embarrassment."

"Who is le Diable?" Caroline asked not understanding the attorney's demeanor.

The professor nodded in affirmation of his friend's suggestion and hurried a bewildered Caroline out of harm's way. Just as they arrived at the stairwell Fredrick Winston bolted out of the elevator doors right next to them.

If looks could kill, Charles Morgan would have been dead on the spot, along with the elegant Caroline Righetti. The vulgar round man looked as if he might actually explode at that very moment with pure violent rage.

"What the hell is going on here? Take your gawdamned filthy hands off my daughter, you son-of-a-bitch!" The angry short man yelled at Chappy with fire in his eyes as spit bubbled and drooled around the red-hot stogy in his mouth.

In an instant, he stepped forward, grabbed Chappy by the suit coat, and threw an off-balance punch at the stunned professor. In the midst of that same clumsy motion, Winston dropped his foul smelling Cuban cigar inside of his own overcoat. The rotund man presented a somewhat comical, yet tragic dance routine as he hopped around on one foot and then the other in an attempt to retrieve the lit cigar from inside his coat. The stogy, burning through his shirt, made Winston even more angry and animated as he tore at his jacket cursing all the while at the top of his voice, "Oh shit! Get the gawdamned thing off me!"

When he finally caught hold of the hot smoking stogy he boorishly threw it onto the beautiful hotel carpet where he left it to smolder. In the blink of an eye Chappy's nemesis turned the lovely evening of celebration into a tragic horror story.

Chappy easily dodged the short man's first blow just as Simon Pearle stepped in between the two men and caught the full force of Winston's second fist squarely on the chin. Mayhem broke out in the luxurious hotel as Simon was knocked out cold and Caroline scrambled to his aid in her chic evening dress and high-heeled slippers. Chappy attempted to subdue the out-of-control Fredrick Winston with little success as the short rotund man continued to shout vulgarities and flail about in the confined public area. Within seconds the hotel staff arrived on scene to subdue the foul-mouthed and belligerent obese man as a gathering of astonished and curious bystanders collected in the hallway.

The entire scene was incredibly vulgar and disconcerting. In a few more minutes, two of the larger hotel staff members finally got Fredrick Winston restrained and escorted him to the elevator as a stunned and moaning Simon Pearle reopened his eyes.

Rubbing his red tinged jaw in obvious pain, Simon moaned.

Dangerous Intentions

"Ooh, la la….Ooh, la la."

Suddenly Caroline rushed toward Winston with her long beautiful dark hair waving behind her like wings. She shoved at him with both arms beating her fists upon his chest. Towering above him she railed "I hate you Fredrick Winston, you're nothing but a bastard and a bully. You are an embarrassment to humanity, you evil filthy old man! This is exactly what you did to my mother and me, and I swear you will never ever touch me again. I hate knowing that you're my father."

Tears began to wash down Caroline's pink flushed cheeks as she continued to confront her biological father. "You mean nothing to me! You haven't been a part of my life since Mama died. You are dead to me. Dead, do you hear me? Dead. Dead. Dead! I never want to see you or hear from you again, do you understand me? Why can't you just leave me alone?"

The shocked crowd of onlookers stood in hushed silence as they witnessed Caroline's tirade and her subsequent collapse into an emotional heap on the floor. She sobbed hysterically at her father's feet. With unusual grace, the vulgar old man held his tongue as he watched his beautiful daughter unravel before his eyes.

Chappy moved quickly to console his lover. Her beautiful floor-length mint-green and beaded evening gown spread around her like frothing sea foam. The professor recognized that she had never looked more beautiful than she did in that heart breaking and tender moment. As Charles swept her into his arms like a small child, she buried her head against his broad shoulders. Caroline wept with uncontrollable sobs.

"I'm sorry Charles. I'm so sorry. Please forgive me. I never wanted you to know about him." Caroline repeated the phrases over and over as the tall blond man held her safely in his arms. In that moment, all he cared about was protecting her from Fredrick Winston at any cost.

Charles Morgan needed Caroline as much as she needed him, if not more. It was perfectly clear to all who observed Chappy and Caroline during those few unfortunate moments that the two of them were kindred spirits and perfectly aligned soul mates.

As the hotel staffers physically hauled the uncooperative Fredrick Winston into the elevator, his demeanor instantly changed back into the hateful and foul-mouthed ogre who had interrupted the happy couple and their silk scarf celebration. He broke free of the staffers' hold on him just long enough to take another wild swing at the dazed Simon Pearle as he leaned against the wall holding his jaw. The punch fell short of its target but Fredrick's vulgar words pierced the silence once again.

"I'll get you Morgan, you son-of-a-bitch. Mark my words. You're going to pay for stealing my little girl. This is your fault, you bastard, I'll ruin you if it's the last thing I do!"

Chapter 15

"I've been pacing for hours just trying to figure this mess out," Charles stated, obviously agitated as he struggled to find the words. "I don't understand why you kept your father's identity a secret from me, Caroline, when he lives right here in the city. And how is it that you are Doctor Caroline Righetti when your given name is Winston? You know how much I hate either of us keeping secrets. I think I deserve an explanation, don't you?" Professor Morgan was bursting at the seams with emotion and he was barely able to keep his frustration in check.

"Yes, Chappy, of course you do," Caroline responded cautiously. "I've intended to tell you who my father is for some time now. But when I learned about the problems he has given your company and the animosity between the two of you, I just couldn't find the right time to bring it up. I certainly didn't want this to come between us, Chappy."

The beautiful doctor moved closer to the man she loved and stated forcefully. "For heaven's sake, Charles, what is wrong with you? I haven't had anything to do with the man for years."

Suddenly irritated beyond measure, Charles responded defiantly, "Who told you I had trouble with Fredrick Winston? I didn't know I was the subject of idle gossip."

Concerned by his sudden agitation, Caroline demanded restraint. "You must stop this interrogation right now Charles Morgan. You are being totally ridiculous and unreasonable. Think for a moment before you speak to me like that! You know me better than that - or have you forgotten everything we've shared for the past few years? Lionel simply mentioned the many difficulties you've had with Fredrick Winston when he and Laurel and I were planning our first silk scarf party together. Lionel had just picked up the silk scarves from the designer and delivered them to me here at home. Laurel was helping with the dinner menu. It was all very innocent, Charles, I assure you," she added trying to clear the air. Caroline moved a bit closer to the professor in an effort to look him in the eye. The couple stood face-to-face for a long, silent, and awkward moment. It seemed like an eternity to Caroline and then an angry Chappy immediately turned away from her gaze.

Young Dr. Righetti spoke again. "We three had tea and biscuits. You know Lionel likes to talk about the things that matter most to him and you are at the top of that list, Charles Morgan, in case you've forgotten. Lionel certainly didn't have any knowledge about who my father is, he learned about it last night just as you did. He was merely concerned about you and the affects that such a horrible man was having on your health and the success of your company." Caroline could see that Chappy was deeply distressed and she was becoming genuinely alarmed by his totally unreasonable attitude. She sensed the emotional barrier that was quickly building around him.

It was a side of the distinguished blond professor's personality that she had never witnessed before. Caroline was suddenly frightened by the stranger who stood before her. His vacant stare burned a hole through her heart.

"Please, Dearest," she pleaded, "You must understand that there was nothing underhanded about my not telling you about that man, my supposed father.

Dangerous Intentions

I was trying to protect us both from his vile behavior. I have spent a great deal of time and energy building a life that he cannot influence or control. It hasn't been easy, I might add, because he's a very influential man. He put pressure on the hospital for information which I have barely managed to keep from him in the first place."

Suddenly aggravated with his apparent indifference, Caroline continued in a strong and determined voice. "Fredrick Winston was furious when he found out that I am legally using the Righetti name, so I know first-hand about how vindictive he can be. He tried without success to get me fired from the hospital staff. He threatened to cut-off my inheritance, which I encouraged him to do, by the way, Charles. I kept this secret from you because I don't want him to hurt me ever again. Simply put, I don't want such a despicable man to ever come between us. I don't know if I could handle that, especially now, Charles."

Still feeling the sting of pride and disappointment about the secrets she had kept, Charles responded indignantly. "What about your name, where does it come from? I can't believe that we have lived together for all these years and I don't have an inkling of who you really are."

Feeling threatened, Caroline crossed her arms tightly to buoy her self-confidence. "Oh come on now, Charles, give me a little credit. You are being utterly bizarre. I'm still the same woman after all. Nothing has changed." "I love you and you love me. *We* are just the same."

Caroline felt anger rising up within her as she watched the look of emotional detachment spread across Chappy's face but she continued speaking anyway. "My mother's name was Anna Marie Righetti. I took her maiden name when I went to college and I had it legally changed when I graduated and entered med school. There's no big mystery here, Charles, I just didn't want to be known as Fredrick Winston's daughter.

Can't you understand that? For heaven's sake, he and my mother had a terrible life together. No amount of money can make up for the way he treated her or me for that matter. I hate him, Charles, honestly. I have hated him for most of my life and I can't think of anything worse than being his daughter."

"This is a very dangerous situation we have stumbled into, Caroline," Chappy stated flatly. "I don't think you fully understand the scope of what it truly means. Your father is a despicable and vengeful man who will stop at nothing to destroy me now that he knows about us. And my company is in grave danger as well. He has proven that time and again over the years. I should have known from the beginning that he is your father. This changes everything, do you hear me, everything."

Befuddled by his strange behavior, Caroline steadied herself behind a large leather recliner in the living room.

Dr. Morgan suddenly began to wring his hands as he paced back and forth in front of Caroline. He began to rant about Fredrick Winston and appeared to be unraveling before her very eyes. "That vile SOB unscrupulously manipulated good people and distorted facts and figures which cost the livelihoods of several of my colleagues in an attempt to get to me. I have several hundred employees to look after now, Caroline, and they're like family to me."

"Fredrick Winston is a monstrous and powerful enemy. He has money and prestige at his disposal and I don't want such corruption to touch their lives in any way." As an after-thought he added sheepishly, "I don't want him to ever hurt you again Caroline. I couldn't live with myself if that happened."

Charles Morgan suddenly sat down in the chair opposite Caroline with his head nestled pitifully in his hands. As she watched him from across the room, her heart ached for this gentle man she lovingly shared her life with. A sudden unexplainable sense of despair quietly passed over her. Caroline was deeply afraid for the first time in her life. For a moment or

Dangerous Intentions

two it seemed that the professor's attitude had softened and that he might be experiencing a change of heart. But with a sense of dread apparent on his face, Chappy merely continued his statement in a more subdued and quiet voice.

"I'm afraid that I cannot protect you, my love, as long as we stay together. Now that this evil man knows where you are and that you and I are together he will stop at nothing to dishonor and break me and my company in an effort to get even because he's lost you. Winston will never accept losing you, Caroline, never as long as he lives. We will never have any peace together. You know that as well as I. He will always blame me for taking you away from him. I can't allow him to hurt you because of me. I could never live with myself if he did. For him to destroy me is one thing, but destroying you or the people who work for me is not an option I am willing to take a chance on."

"What are you saying Chappy?" Caroline asked suddenly more afraid. "Are you telling me we're through, that you are giving up on our relationship all because Fredrick Winston is my biological father?"

Caroline drew near to Charles and knelt in front of him. With tears in her eyes she pleaded with him.

"Please, Charles, I beg of you. Don't consider such a drastic move for even a moment. We can do this together, Chappy. He can't hurt us as long as we're together. I love you. I don't want to lose you. Please, please, I beg of you, don't throw us away."

Chapter 16

Charles Morgan spent a restless night in a desperately agitated state after the humiliating fiasco with Fredrick Winston ruined the silk scarf celebration he and Caroline so happily enjoyed. The unexpected news regarding her father's identity was a stunning turn of events. The more Chappy thought about Fredrick Winston the madder he became. His stomach was tied in knots. His thoughts were dark and brooding and his judgment was clouded with a range of extreme emotions. He was furious....furious with Winston, furious with himself, and even more furious with Caroline for keeping her birthright a secret.

He was also consumed with guilt, confusion, and disbelief. His sudden overpowering doubt regarding his relationship with the lovely Caroline Righetti blindsided him and smacked of a selfish and narrow-mindedness which privately embarrassed him.

Paralyzed by his own arrogance, Charles Morgan was disappointed and intolerant and so very, very angry. It was the anger he couldn't seem to get a handle on. Chappy adored Caroline and he truly loved her. She had opened the door to a new world of love and affection that he never experienced before. But that door suddenly slammed shut with a fury he

Dangerous Intentions

had not predicted. He did not like surprises and was ill-prepared to deal with them. He was a man of discipline and order and this emotional turmoil was messy and unpredictable. Methodical details in a controlled environment were his specialty and his lifeline.

The world as he knew it had been destroyed in an instant. And Chappy feared he would not recover emotionally in spite of his own personal regret. Fredrick Winston, the belligerent and insufferable man whom he had literally grown to hate, had finally forced his way in to the professor's life in the most dramatic sense possible. Chappy was completely devastated by that realization.

Charles Morgan was exceptionally annoyed with his reality, which at its very core barely camouflaged the deep and painful agony he was also feeling. As an overwhelming sense of betrayal swept through him like an ice cold wind there was nothing to be said......he was shattered.

Chapter 17

Caroline Righetti was distraught. Her night had been extremely restless and she was near exhaustion from very little sleep. The beautiful doctor was unable to wrap her mind around Chappy's unreasonable response to news about her father's identity. He seemed callous and unfeeling and she no longer saw the look of unconditional love in his eyes. He became a stranger to her overnight, and the entire unpleasant episode felt surreal in the morning sun. She loved Charles Morgan with her entire being but it was apparent that his attitude toward her had dramatically changed in the course of a few hours. She was thoroughly disgusted with his behavior. Flabbergasted and disillusioned, she was nearly sick with worry.

He was angry. She was defensive and fearful. She sensed the private world they built together slip away and there was nothing she could do or say to stop its sad demise. The man she loved seemed unable or unwilling to grasp the fact that Caroline was estranged from her father and wanted nothing to do with him. The young doctor had found her own way in spite of her parents and she was naturally proud of herself.

She had mistakenly assumed that Charles Morgan understood her accomplishments and admired her choices.

She felt foolish and victimized in light of his thoughtless over-reaction.

Caroline believed that Chappy was behaving like a selfish and spoiled child who couldn't have his own way. It was ridiculous and unsettling. It was totally beyond any adult behavior she could imagine. They loved one another, for heaven's sake – what could possibly be more important than that? Their relationship was built on trust and mutual respect, and yet suddenly it seemed to have all vanished overnight.

An overwhelming sense of dread swept through her as sadness filled her heart. If there had been room left for anger she would have been mad as hell. Sadly, the years that she and Chappy happily spent together in love and adoration melted away leaving her depressed, weary, and terribly alone.

Chapter 18

Days later Doctor Charles Morgan quietly put the wheels of change into motion. He met with Simon Pearle who would have the necessary legal documents ready at week's end. There were to be no loose ends and nothing left to chance. He purchased a large and beautiful new house in a secure gated compound overlooking the Monterey Bay and set up a substantial trust fund in Caroline's name for her continued care and support in the event that anything untoward might happen to him. Unobtrusive body guards were hired to provide additional surveillance and security around the clock which would remain in place as long as deemed necessary. Simon Pearle would see to those details personally.

Chappy selected and purchased a new car, something he had not done in the years since Lionel became his personal driver. He chose a 1963 Gold Studebaker Avanti. Chappy learned through his stockbroker that Studebaker was rumored to stop production of their classic automobiles within the year and in an impulsive moment he decided he needed to have just such a car of his own to drive. Along with the beautiful new sporty car, Chappy made arrangements to have six million dollars cash in untraceable bills delivered to him.

The money was to come from his personal savings accounts. He was cutting his ties swiftly which he hoped would thoroughly distress Fredrick Winston and convince him to end his futile disagreement with the professor.

Lionel Carver was to receive the deed to Chappy's home in San Francisco and the titles to three automobiles along with a stipend of two million dollars for himself and his wife, Laurel Saint James. Chappy intended for the elderly couple to travel and have some much deserved rest and relaxation after their long and dedicated years of service. He would surprise them with the gift after his meeting with Caroline in a few days.

Chappy's company was placed in a secure trust with Pearle and Associates where Simon would manage and direct the new research projects and follow the existing contracts to completion.

Charles Morgan added a surprising caveat to the legal documents which stunned Simon Pearle: After twenty years, in the year 1983, the entire elite company that Chappy worked so diligently to build was to be sold to the company's most loyal and vested employees for the purchase price of five-thousand-dollars each.

It was an amazing offer for the multi-million dollar engineering facility and its employees. All company profits were to be reinvested in research and design for the first ten years until 1973. Profits would then be divided between Caroline Righetti and Simon Pearle (or their survivors) for the remaining ten years until the sale to employees was completed in 1983.

With the company's name change and the change of management there would be no loopholes for Fredrick Winston to interfere with its new legal status. And perhaps there would be no further need for the arrogant short man to pursue the disruption of research under Simon's direction. Chappy had complete faith and trust in Simon Pearle.

The French attorney had more than proved himself to be competent, loyal, and discreet, both as a lawyer and a friend.

The funds from the Morgan Shipping business in Boston would remain invested for perpetuity with endowments to the ballet and philharmonic as well as several private universities. Charles Preston Morgan made changes that he believed would most protect and benefit the ones he loved.

Chapter 19

Caroline arrived home from the hospital looking pale and worried while Chappy was working at his desk. She sensed that he was in a dark mood by the deep frown on his face and she suddenly feared the worst.

"Is there something wrong, Chappy?" she asked with genuine concern. "Are you not feeling well? You look terrible. You have dark circles around your eyes and your color isn't good. Let me fix you a cup of tea. I bought some of the English biscuits you like, I'll get us some. I know I could certainly use a boost myself."

"Please hush, Caroline," Charles responded as he reached for her hand. "Just sit down here a minute. I'm fine, really I am. I just have a lot on my mind that I need to speak to you about. Please, just sit down here next to me and let me talk."

Caroline, anxious and uncomfortable, loosened her jacket and sat down in the elegant 17th Century carved oak armchair next to the desk. She hated to see Chappy in such a mood again because there had been little she could do to shake him out of it in the past.

Chappy began to speak as a matter of fact. "I bought a new house in Monterey that I want you to live in, Caroline. It's a beautiful big new place with large windows and magnificent views of the sea. I'm sure you'll love it as much as I do the minute you see it. It has several lovely flower gardens and a wide covered deck all around. There are windswept trees and large granite boulders that protect it on two sides. I think it's nearly a perfect location. I know it will add time onto your commute to the hospital, but I think the benefits far outweigh the negatives."

Pausing just a moment he continued. "I am giving this old house to Lionel and Laurel. They deserve a rest and I can't think of anyone who would take better care of this grand place than the two of them. I am leaving the company in the capable hands of Simon and his associates and I'm going to take a little time off. I do hope this meets with your approval and satisfaction."

Feeling hopeful for the first time in days, Caroline responded, "I think it sounds wonderful, Chappy. It's about time you took a break. Maybe we can go on a trip somewhere, maybe a nice long cruise. I have vacation time I can schedule and a good rest would do us both a world of good. I know that I'm more than ready for a change. I'm just surprised that you haven't mentioned this to me before. I love Monterey, but you're making a lot of decisions without consulting me and I thought we were partners."

The light-hearted mood she was feeling suddenly began to dissipate as Caroline became uncomfortable with the totally vacant look in Chappy's eyes. They were no longer the eyes of love that had gazed upon her with devotion. They were no longer the eyes of her soul mate and kindred spirit. His cobalt blue eyes appeared to be void of any emotion whatsoever. Caroline's hopes were crushed.

"Does this have anything to do with that new car in the garage?" she asked.

"Are you having an affair?" Chappy shook his head, responding in the negative without saying a single word.

Afterward Caroline gasped ever so slightly and quickly covered her mouth with her palm. A moment later, more composed, she asked, "Well then, is this some sort of emotional or personal crisis, Charles that you are afraid to tell me about? Are you ill? What is it Charles? You're not acting like yourself at all and quite frankly you're scaring me to death."

"No, it's not an emotional crisis," he shrugged. "I'm just trying to do what's best for you, for both of us really and the company too if that's possible. This new hullabaloo involving Fredrick Winston has caused me to rethink my plans for the future. I don't want to make any mistakes where you are concerned, Caroline. You simply must try and understand that I need to do this."

Caroline quietly added, "I love you, Charles Morgan, I truly do. And I've never known you to make a single mistake."

"I love you too, Caroline," the professor said quietly almost letting his emotions rise to the surface. "I love you with all my heart. I hope and pray that this is the best thing for all of us." Clearing his throat, Charles continued as a matter of fact. "This is the key to the new house. It's located on a bluff overlooking the sea. It's a private place where you'll be safe. Winston will have a difficult time getting to you there. I have arranged for the movers to come day after tomorrow. You are free to pick and choose what furniture you want to take out of this house and free to buy whatever else you might want or need to make the new house a cozy home for yourself. Whatever you don't want from here I'm sure Laurel will keep or she can give it to someone who needs it. For anything else that you need, Caroline, please contact Simon. He has my authorization to assist you in any way possible. He's a very good man and you can always count on him."

Dumfounded, stunned, and heart broken by his total lack of emotion, Caroline began to cry softly. "Is that it? Just like that can you cut me out of your life with one easy stroke of the pen?

What are you really talking about here Chappy? Are you going somewhere without me? Are you leaving me to run off around the world like my father did to me and like your father did to you? Tell me right now what's going on with you? You're not moving into the new house with me are you?" she asked fearing the answer.

"Talk to me, please, Charles," she begged. "You sound so cold and distant. Just tell me the truth. That's the least I deserve! What's going on with you?"

Silently Charles Morgan calmly put on his coat and picked up his suitcase. He wiped a few stray tears from Caroline's cheek and kissed her gently on the lips for a long tender moment. Hesitating ever so slightly, as if he might change his mind and come to his senses, he turned away slowly and walked out of the door. In a quiet defining moment he closed yet another chapter of his life's story and never looked back.

"Chappy, don't do this," Caroline cried. "We can work this out. I'm begging you, please don't do this."

Chapter 20

Lionel was waxing the Rolls Royce when Chappy left his beautiful old house on the hill for the last time. Emotions that had been held in restraint with Caroline rushed to the surface as he paused to speak to his old friend. Tears welled in his eyes and then rolled silently down his cheeks.

"Lionel, I have some good news for you, my old friend. You're fired." Chappy continued fighting back tears. "From now on you and Laurel will be the owners of this magnificent old house. I want you to live here and take good care of her as I know you will. Doctor Righetti will be moving in a few days and I know you will extend her every courtesy just as you have for me all these years."

Chappy paused, pulled a handkerchief out of his pocket, and blew his nose. "I want you to have these three cars, Lionel. Enjoy them and drive the hell out of them! Here are the titles and the keys to the house, and this is your bank account with a little spending money for you and Laurel to enjoy. Thank you, Lionel. You've been a very loyal companion and a very good friend."

Lionel was flabbergasted and caught totally off-guard. He could barely speak. "Oh, Mr. Charles," he stammered. "Mr. Charles, I'm overwhelmed. I don't know what to say."

As Chappy hugged his old friend, big tears began to roll silently down his cheeks again. It was the first time since he had left the Commonwealth of Massachusetts that he allowed himself to cry. His wonderful and happy life in San Francisco was over.

"There's no need to say anything, Lionel," Chappy added, rubbing his old friend's back. "You deserve this and more. Goodbye, old friend and God bless you."

"God bless you too, Mr. Charles," Lionel said struggling against his own tears and the lump that developed in his throat. "Thank you so very much for your kindness, Sir, it means the world to me. It's been my honor and pleasure to work for you, Mr. Charles. You are a fine gentleman. I'll see to it that Doctor Righetti has everything she needs. You can count on me."

Chapter 21

Earlier that same day, in a sentimental moment of emotional weakness, the professor hastily grabbed two items from his home that personally reminded him of Caroline. In the backseat and trunk of his new car along with a few clothes and several large bags of money were boxes of empty notebooks, a box of household items, and several cooking utensils. But safely wrapped inside of several soft towels lay one of the delicate Tiffany lamps Caroline brought with her on the day she moved in with him. A matching set had belonged to her mother, Anna, and was one of her favorite treasures.

Chappy always felt connected to Caroline and her family history each time she spoke about her mother as she touched the lamps with tenderness and affection. The mere thought of never seeing Caroline Righetti again and never being near her was simply unbearable. He had shared Caroline's precious memories of her beloved mother, Anna Righetti, and Caroline had trusted him to keep the memories safe and private. He couldn't help himself. He simply had to have one of the lamps with him wherever it was that the gold Avanti took him. He needed a piece of Caroline's heart to stay alive and whole and to help keep Anna's memory safe.

The professor acted totally on impulse for the second sentimental item that was safely tucked away in his coat pocket. It was something he had taken from Caroline's dressing table with a sense of desperation only moments before she returned home from the hospital. It was the beautiful hand-painted silk scarf that had flown through the air and into his life four years earlier. The silk scarf was the beginning of Caroline, elegant Caroline, the love of his life. He simply had to keep it with him always.

Chappy Morgan drove through his beloved City by the Bay not knowing where he might end up. His mind was a blur. It was the end of all he knew. He was a man without purpose or destination for the first time in his adult life.

The sporty new gold Avanti purred like a kitten and handled extremely well as he left the city and headed east. In his haste to leave Fredrick Winston and his league of goons, Chappy suddenly remembered that he had failed to register his new automobile or to even obtain a current driver's license. This oversight, as simple as it seemed, would ultimately prove to be a blessing in disguise.

With the wind blowing through his blond curly hair and the temporary dealership papers flapping vigorously in the wind, Chappy pushed the gold sports car past the speed limit on US Hwy. 40 and raced toward the rest of his life. The brilliant man was numbed with emotion. He was totally lost in his own misery. There was no hope left in his life and no promise for the future. He had given up. He was defeated.

Chapter 22

The cold Nevada wind was howling as tall and handsome Chappy Morgan lifted the kerosene lamp from the rock fireplace mantle. Just as he grabbed for it a powerful clap of thunder broke directly overhead.

During these early months after his arrival in the remote high desert of Nevada, the professor was ill-prepared for the sudden thunderstorms that often developed near the abandoned town of Stillwater, Nevada. He was uneasy with the sudden darkness from such annoying power outages.

The professor had already spent months looking over his shoulder, expecting trouble to rear its ugly head at any moment. His own tangled professional life had not yet caught up with him nor had it begun to set him free. As a consequence, he constantly searched for any desperate character from his past that might unexpectedly appear.

Enraged yet embarrassed, he shuddered slightly with the intense rumble of thunder and grumbled that he was still totally out of his element in the rustic setting. Hard as he might try, he was still just a forty-five-year-old city boy at heart. As lightening flashed for a second time across the Nevada sky, he was quickly caught off-guard when the shadow of a stranger appeared outside and hastily passed by the window headed toward the cabin's front door. Luckily, the power outage and the room's dark interior shielded him from the stranger's view. But it quickly became apparent that the professor was in need of much more than luck. His past was finally about to come knocking. In a curious state of panic, Charles Morgan grabbed for the first thing he could find to defend himself and then he slipped quietly out the side door in an attempt to follow behind the dark figure.

His pulse was racing as blood pounded at his temple. Nervous and anxious, he quietly inched along the outside wall of his adobe cabin. Pure adrenaline propelled him forward as he carefully avoided the loose squeaky boards positioned along the wooden walkway surrounding the cabin. Chappy quickly assessed the situation as being risky and dire. He was definitely in over his head. After all, he had been a refined and educated scientist for most of his life and now here he was slinking along in the dark with fear and trepidation.

Was it more than he bargained for he wondered. How far could he actually go with his plan to completely disappear? Was he strong enough and bold enough to really make that happen? There was little time for his introspective thoughts, however, as the wind whipped fiercely around his barren yard and up the side of his modest house. Small pieces of debris tumbled in all directions as the wind eddied among the broken-down outbuildings. With each gust of wind, the remnants of his old outhouse door banged back and forth against the abandoned toilet as its hinges screeched with complaint.

Rain drops mixed with sleet pelted him like stinging projectiles and yet he felt a strange sense of exhilaration and extreme terror all in the same moment. Chappy Morgan was about to come of age in the real Wild West that previously he had only read about in history books. It was destined to be a life changing moment.

Just ahead of him Professor Morgan could see the stranger.

Dangerous Intentions

The dark figure rounded the front corner of the adobe building as another flash of lightening lit up the moonless night sky. Chappy stopped dead still for a second or two certain that the stranger would see him lurking behind. But that was not the case as the professor quickly realized.

With a few more steps Chappy could see the man's slim outline leaning against the front door as if he were trying to glean what or whom might lie in wait for him on the interior side of the wood barricade. The unwelcome stranger hesitated for a moment to adjust his Fedora in an attempt to shield his face against the relentless wind and horizontal rain. That single moment of hesitation proved to be the stranger's undoing and miraculously became Chappy's greatest advantage.

As if he were part of a choreographed dance routine, the professor quickly gathered his weight, held his breath, and charged on near tip-toes toward the man. He acknowledged the sudden flash of a silver hand gun and then swung the heavy iron skillet into the back of the stranger's head with all the strength he could muster. It was a perfect grand slam hit. It all happened in one smooth, easy, and rhythmic movement and was finished in seconds. It was glorious. But when the choreography ended the stranger was sprawled out on the front porch bleeding profusely from his ears and nose. Hovering in the darkness, wet and cold, Chappy heard the man's last gasp for breath. The stranger lay dead at the professor's feet and it had only taken one single blow to the back of his head with the heavy cast iron skillet.

Morgan's historic old outhouse and the deep pit beneath it were finally put to use after the thunderstorm abated.

His first real physical struggle was to remove the outsider's body from the porch by himself. Lifting the stranger's dead weight was terribly awkward as Morgan soon discovered. It was impossible for him to pick up the man and carry him by himself. After some additional thought, the professor managed to move the corpse by rolling it onto a tarp and simply pulling it across his yard.

Before the dead body was finally dumped into the outhouse pit, Chappy felt self-conscious about undressing the stranger. For some unknown reason it seemed important for him to remove the man's clothing. He actually did so with his eyes in a squint most of the time because the stranger's nakedness became a very personal and embarrassing thing to the professor. It disrupted his train of thought and left him feeling more than slightly unbalanced by his awkward invasion of the man's privacy.

Charles Morgan made no attempt to discern the dead man's identity. He simply tossed the stranger's unopened wallet into the dark pit without ever looking inside. Right or wrong, he couldn't bear to know whose life he so easily snuffed out and he presumed it would make things easier in the future. He did keep the silver handgun, however. It turned out to be a 1963 Browning semi-automatic pistol.

It was important for the professor to remain focused as there was still work to be done. It became obvious that the partially rotted bags of lye left for years near the outhouse had been left behind for this exact morbid purpose. Chappy made the decision to use the lye without a moment's hesitation. But dragging the heavy bags of lye through the darkness and fresh mud became extremely difficult simply because his emotional condition was rapidly deteriorating.

The brilliant man had reduced his educated life to the most banal of survival instincts befitting a warrior. He was badly shaken by his own actions and his personal disregard for human life. It appeared he was on the verge of a psychotic break whether he recognized that fact or not.

The professor was not accustomed to such heavy manual labor and thus his movements were extremely slow and cautious. His muscles cramped and his heart raced before he finally accomplished his task.

Charles Morgan later moved the stranger's olive green and yellow four-door '57 Chevy Bel Air to an isolated corner of his property surrounded by sagebrush and heavy salt cedar. He doused it thoroughly with gasoline he syphoned from his gold Avanti. The car burned quietly for hours in the pitch black darkness until dawn broke over the Stillwater Mountains. As he watched the last of the smoke rise from the charred metal skeleton, Chappy considered the consequences of his actions. Perhaps this was to become the symbolic burning bridge that he crossed much too eagerly. Thoughts of Caroline swirled in his head......this was not what he wanted, not by a long shot. But in another defining moment of his life it became his destiny.

A few days later, the burned-out shell of the '57 Chevy was left to rust in the salt grass and alkali. On a whim, the professor cleverly turned the black and yellow California license plate, number 5KGQ436, into a perfect roof for a bird house which he kept in his yard as an eerie reminder of his terrible deed. The Fedora and the slim man's expensive imported clothes were made into a fairly attractive albeit skinny scarecrow to stand watch over Chappy's shabby vegetable garden.

Chappy's new found life continued day after day without distraction. No one came to his high desert oasis looking for the stranger in the '57 Chevy and no one came to hold Chappy Morgan accountable for the life he had extinguished.

However briefly it may have been, Charles P. Morgan felt a twinge of personal sadness that not a single being cared enough about the stranger's life to even search for him. Although the man's neglect made things extremely simple for the professor, it seemed a melancholy statement about the man's life.

Chappy Morgan's slow descent into hell began quietly during that stormy summer night. But it soon became evident that his uninterrupted slide into the dark abyss would become inescapable. The extreme depth to which his misery was destined to fall became both steady and deliberate.

Chapter 23

Professor Morgan was settling into his reclusive lifestyle as the second summer made its way to the high Nevada desert. After more than a year in his hideaway, he barely recognized his own face in the mirror. His long blond hair hung several inches below his collar and the shaggy blond beard that grew from so many months of not shaving gave him a totally homeless look. He was beginning to fade away from society with very little effort and was actually becoming comfortable in his own neglected skin. It was an odd concept for him to give up his professional life in such a strange manner and yet it was becoming more and more natural for him each day. His old familiar likeness was disappearing along with his past.

Not long after his arrival in the Lahontan Valley, the professor discovered he had a talent for drawing with pencil and paper. His sketches became uncommonly good for a novice with no previous experience or interest and it seemed there were not enough hours in the day for him to capture everything he wanted to save on paper. He became obsessed with his sketches. His appetite for subjects to draw could not be quenched. It was a compulsion.

He became lost in his thoughts and spent every day searching the Stillwater National Wildlife Refuge, studying the

Dangerous Intentions

migrating water fowl, and capturing every moment in one sketch or another. San Francisco drifted farther and farther away from his life but not so the painful thoughts of Caroline Righetti.

That was, however, until a seemingly innocent horn honked non-stop in the distance one cool morning. Unbeknownst to him, Chappy's life was destined to spiral out of control once again. With anxiety writhing in his stomach, the professor suddenly forced himself back into reality with a clear and focused awareness that something was awry. He picked up an unused red brick from his yard as he strolled cautiously down his long winding driveway toward the main road in search of the noisy horn. A strange voice called out to him just as the honking stopped. "Howdy partner, unusually cool morning isn't it?"

Immediately Chappy knew that trouble was lurking just outside his newly locked gate. Without responding, he approached closer to the stranger on the far side of the fence until he could see clearly that it was most certainly an enemy. The figure standing outside of Chappy's gate was none other than Ho Chan Wang, a well-known gangster from San Francisco's Chinatown who was undoubtedly sent to find Charles Morgan by some of the goons Caroline's father had employed. He was certain of it. He recognized Chan from previous television news reports and newspaper photographs he had seen in San Francisco. Ironically, Chan's Chinese name when translated into English meant "for the good" but there wasn't a single good thing about the hired thug. Chappy knew the man's evil reputation very well.

Hatred for Fredrick Winston raged inside of Chappy's being until the mere thought of the insufferable banker was more than he could possibly bear. The professor knew that Chan was a violent member of the Chinese underground who had a reputation for highly paid murder-for-hire plots.

His attacks had been made against a variety of wealthy businessmen and their families on numerous occasions. Suddenly self-preservation kicked in with a vengeance as Chappy remembered Fredrick Winston.

Images of the rotund man instantly tangled together in Chappy's mind along with indiscriminate and unwanted memories of his own father, Lester Morgan. At that very moment in time it was impossible to discern which man he actually hated more. His vision was definitely clouded along with his judgment. He knew Caroline's father could no longer hurt him personally but the same would never be said about the hired goons on Winston's payroll who might try to make a name for them self. Chappy suddenly became enraged and trapped in a moment of dangerous intentions.

Ho Chan Wang was momentarily caught by surprise with the distorted visual image that Charles Morgan presented. He did not immediately recognize the professor and thus let himself get careless. It was a stupid mistake in judgment and one that would cost the Asian dearly.

Chappy feigned a serious stumble, which allowed him to distract his enemy as he heaved the heavy brick with all his might at the unwanted man. Because of the Asian's arrogance and careless disregard for his surroundings, the red brick slammed into Ho Chan's face. Bewildered by the surprise attack, Chan staggered, cursed, and fell to his knees protecting his bloodied head. Chappy unlocked the gate and rushed to clobber the man's head again and again with the red brick.

Chan lost consciousness.

Chappy lost control.

In his misplaced rage, the professor completely forgot about the Browning pistol that was tucked safely inside the deep pocket of his bibbed overalls. It was rage that propelled him forward and pure hatred that ultimately insured his survival.

He was consumed with fear and confusion.

Chappy clumsily dumped the unresponsive Asian into the back of the man's own red and white 1959 El Camino truck. He then drove the vehicle onto his property after quickly relocking the gate. The classic vehicle was well maintained and immaculate. The professor was impressed. Chappy quickly admired the batwing-like fins of the '59 Chevrolet with its highly polished chrome as he ran his fingers over the sleek truck body.

This was a totally unexpected turn of events. The professor had once again hastily reacted rather than consider the situation with appropriate comprehension. Dr. Charles Morgan's life had indeed regressed to the most basic need of personal survival. All humanity be damned!

Chappy struggled with Chan's unconscious body as he fought to remove it from the bed of the El Camino. His indecision about what to do with Ho Chan Wang was short lived, however, as the feisty Asian regained consciousness and lunged at the professor like a cornered snake.

Chappy was no match for the quick karate moves and physical agility of the younger man. Morgan was soft and out of shape after so many months in his reclusive haven. He was knocked to the ground several times as he grunted and groaned during many unsuccessful attempts to escape the man's grasp.

Thoughts raced through Chappy's mind. If only he could get to the Browning pistol bulging in his pocket. But on second thought he'd had no practice using the weapon and presumed that Wang was probably an expert marksman. None of that really mattered in the heat of the moment.

He was being out-maneuvered by the feisty Aisan in spite of the man's bleeding head wound. As luck would have it, Chappy's six-feet-two-inches in height proved to be an advantage over the shorter Aisan. Somehow the professor was finally able to break free of the man's choking grasp and roll onto his back gasping for air.

He gave Ho Chan Wang one good solid kick to the groin and heard the distinctive and agonizing smack of his foot against the Asian's genitals. The unwanted guest roiled in pain as he grabbed himself in an attempt to soothe his aching testicles.

Anger and pure hatred exploded on his dark-eyed face as Ho Chan lunged forward toward Chappy once again. Chan's intense pain apparently threw him off-balance just enough during the violent rage that his concentration was sorely diminished. And as a result, during one of his rapidly twirling drop-and-roll maneuvers, he impaled himself on a nearby pitchfork which ceremoniously slid to the ground during the struggle just as Charles P. Morgan rolled out of harm's way. The long tines drove through the Asian's neck nearly severing his head from his torso and he was killed instantly. Suddenly it was all over. The professor heard the last of Ho Chan's blood and oxygen gurgle from his wounds. As suddenly as the fight for his life began - it was over. Chappy's world grew very quiet once again and the Browning pistol remained safely out of sight.

Charles Morgan lay in the dirt for several moments in order to regain his strength. He could not believe his good fortune. He was exhausted. He was euphoric. He was a complete stranger to himself. As his heart raced and his warm breath swirled in the cool morning air, it became clear to Dr. Morgan that he would never again be able to reclaim his past. His days with the lovely Caroline Righetti were gone forever. Men had perished by his hand and there would be consequences.

The tortured body of Ho Chan Wang was buried in the alkali dirt on Chappy's property a good distance away from the adobe cabin. The professor impolitely wrapped the corpse in a carpet remnant and unceremoniously rolled it into a fairly shallow grave.

He recited no poetry, spoke no apologies or regrets, and shed no tears.

The body remained undisturbed for a month or two until the coyotes dug it up sometime later. Out of some misplaced and warped sense of respect, Chappy retrieved the man's skull and wrapped it in a burlap sack. He uncharacteristically saved the skull as if it was his personal trophy.

It became glaringly obvious to the emotionally bankrupt professor that very few remnants of the formerly successful and distinguished Charles Preston Morgan, PhD. were visible on that day. That man had all but vanished from the earth. Every trace of his former educated and sophisticated life had been culled from his soul.

The rest of the Asian's clothes and bones, or what was left of them after the scavengers finished with them, were eventually scattered across the many acres of alkali and salt grass that Chappy owned.

The 1959 El Camino was buried completely intact in its own private grave inside the boundaries of Morgan's land. The professor could not bring himself to actually burn the exquisite vehicle as he had the Chevrolet Bel Air, and it took him several days to dig the necessary pit deep enough to hide it. With the last shovel full of dirt thrown upon the burial site, however, Chappy Morgan chuckled at a bit of irony as he remembered that *El Camino* translated from Spanish meant *the road*. Ho Chan Wang and his beautiful red and white El Camino had certainly traveled to the end of the road. Chappy had seen to that.

The hot-rod red and white truck remains in its resting place on Chappy's property. Although it was buried in its original glory, it is no doubt turning to rust and has become home to some of the dark earth's most undesirable creatures and pests. Ho Chan Wang, a disgusting human who committed horrendous acts for money, merely disappeared from the face of the Earth. No one looked for him and not one single individual mourned his passing. The Asian stranger died a ghastly death and only one lonely man knew the gut-wrenching details.

Chappy's life was totally out of control as his soul spiraled deeper into the depths of despair once again. Fate selected Charles Morgan to give permanent residence to the ghosts of more than one unfortunate stranger. He did so for more than forty years, but at what cost?

Chapter 24

A few years later, on a hot summer morning just after sunrise, Joe and Harry the first pair of mongrel dogs that adopted Chappy Morgan began to bark furiously. They had taken up residence under the porch of his adobe cabin and were very protective of their host.

Harry, a one-hundred-twenty-pound Malamute mix was the dominant alpha male and his size alone made him very intimidating. Joe was a large and more docile neutered male Boxer that followed Harry everywhere with devotion and obedience.

It was unusually warm that day and Chappy allowed himself to sleep late in his cool bedroom. By this hour of the morning he was typically on his way to bird watch. But he hadn't slept very well during the night because a couple of pesky mosquitoes kept buzzing near him threatening an attack. Chappy hated mosquitoes and they were widespread around the wildlife refuge. The bothersome mosquitoes were the main disadvantage to living so near the shallow ponds and marshy wetlands of Stillwater Point Reservoir.

The reclusive Morgan was startled awake by the loud racket the dogs made. Suddenly alarmed by their announcement of unidentified danger, the professor jerked on his boots and grabbed the Browning pistol from the makeshift table near his bed. He muttered to himself about letting his guard down and something about being too complacent in his safe surroundings.

Life had been easy for him the last couple of years and Chappy nearly forgot about his violent past. He liked the rock-solid and steady rhythm of his life and he did not welcome unexpected changes. People always brought changes with them whenever they were present in his life. For that reason alone, and above all else, he did not want people around. The ghosts kept him company alright, but they were peaceful and predictable. He never had to worry about changes where they were concerned.

Joe and Harry ratcheted up their constant barking. It was out of the ordinary for them to make a fuss because Chappy's secluded world was generally bathed in quiet solitude. This was a disruption he did not want on the day he planned to observe and draw the Ruddy Duck drake. He was frustrated with the interruption, to say the least. Wearing only his long johns and boots, Chappy quickly opened the front door of his cabin in time to see a pock-faced black man dressed in leather throw a rock at Harry.

His aim was off as the husky animal growled and crouched closer. As the stranger bent to pick up a stick, Harry charged the man with teeth bared. Chappy aimed the Browning pistol and squeezed the trigger just as the man straightened in time to glance the professor in the doorway and the huge dog leaping through the air. There was not a moment's hesitation or a single question asked. Chappy Morgan simply shot the stranger between the eyes and he suddenly lay dead on the very spot where he stood only moments earlier.

The professor was shocked by his lucky shot as he intended to merely halt the stranger's forward motion with a warning. And Harry's ungodly racket was silenced when the man's body slumped to the ground. Chappy had never fired the 1963 Browning semi-automatic pistol before and he was stunned into total disbelief as he stood in the doorway staring at the stranger's dead body.

What now he thought silently? It all happened so quickly and so easily that he wasn't prepared for such an inconvenient outcome. Morgan assumed the gun shot would merely serve as a warning to the stranger and discourage him from invading his space, but instead he misjudged his own abilities. Once more he simply reacted with survival in mind.

Joe and Harry pranced around the corpse investigating the man dressed in leather. They sniffed and pawed at blood oozing from his head wound. As Chappy regained his composure, he scolded the two mongrel dogs and admonished them back under the porch away from the man's body. What now he asked of himself again as he re-entered his home? It was a perplexing problem for him to dispose of a body in broad daylight and he shrugged at the inopportune timing of it all.

Chappy paused for a moment in front of his dusty mirror. It was something he rarely did these days as the reflection he observed was of no one he knew. A stranger's face always looked back at him and it was disconcerting, to say the least. In the blink of an eye his life had changed forever on that spring evening in San Francisco so long ago. A lifetime ago it seemed to him now – and he would never be the same.

As Chappy faced the stranger in the mirror, he reached out to touch his reflection to be sure it wasn't an illusion or something more sinister. But it was indeed his face. In that desperate moment Chappy prayed that he was delusional and completely out of touch with reality. But this was truly the sad reality of his life.

And it was one he was not at all happy with. Charles Morgan, wearing his usual long johns and bibbed overalls, casually stepped over the dead body in his front yard with Joe and Harry close on his heels. He walked out to the main road after unlocking his gate. There wasn't a vehicle in sight for miles so how did the stranger arrive at his secluded property?

What did he want? Who sent him? All manner of questions swirled in the recluse's mind. Chappy wandered around on the main road outside his gate for a few minutes until something on the side of the road caught his attention. In a small culvert, protected by tall grass and sage, lay a blue and black motorcycle. Suddenly the man dressed in leather made more sense to the weary professor. Upon closer inspection, Chappy determined the bike to be a Triumph T120 Bonneville – a 1965 model.

As Morgan rolled the heavy motorcycle inside the boundary of his property, his thoughts drifted to another time and place many years earlier when he was a college student at Stanford University. Chappy rode a vintage Harley-Davidson motorcycle in those days and was very popular with the young female students on campus. Sunny California had proved the perfect location for such an adventurous activity and he loved feeling the wind blow through his hair and the unfettered freedom the motorcycle represented. He vaguely remembered one particular long-legged and busty brunette in tight shorts who loved to ride with him. Suddenly smiling and struggling to remember the details of her person he asked aloud, "What was her name?"

The sound of his voice triggered an immediate response from Joe and Harry as they wagged their tails in approval. They were perfectly happy to accompany Chappy down the long and winding driveway back to the security of their home. Although he was swept up in a nostalgic moment thinking of his past, the vision of the deceased pock-faced man lying in front of his cabin shook him back to reality abruptly.

There was nothing do be done with the marvelous Triumph Bonneville except to destroy it. Although he toyed with the idea of keeping the cycle for himself, Chappy knew it was impossible and impractical. There was too much risk involved for him to become sentimental at this point and time. After all, he had given up Caroline Righetti. There was nothing else he could lose that would ever compare to the loss he already felt.

Chappy rolled the beautiful motorcycle into the midst of the scavenged junk he had gathered earlier in the week from along the boundaries of his land. This most recent collection of stuff had been added to the constantly growing rusted graveyard on his property like usual. The junkyard was filled with all manner of man's unwanted machinery.

Chappy parked the Triumph next to the rusting hulk of a classic Harley-Davidson motorcycle that was nearly hidden from view. Ironically there were several motorcycle skeletons in the pile when he bought the place. He calmly siphoned the gas out of the tank and set the bike ablaze. It tugged at his heartstrings to watch the fine machine burn in the morning sun. The leather seat, saddlebags, and paint burned quickly along with the tires. Eventually only the skeleton of the formerly beautiful Triumph stood amidst the junk in his collection. It blended in so well that no one would notice. It was just one more member of the graveyard, the large family of rusted steel, worthless engines, and rotted wagons nobody wanted. Finally, Chappy turned his attention to the motorcycle's owner.

As Mr. Morgan began to drag the stranger's body down a small incline toward his slash pile, he noticed a bunch of keys hanging on a long chain attached to the man's leather chaps. They made a jingling sound as the body bumped along the uneven earth. As Chappy rolled the man onto his stomach to remove the bundle of keys, he also noticed that the name *Jangles* was carved into the leather belt the pock-faced man wore.

Without any warning the professor became hysterical.

Even Joe and Harry took notice when the normally quiet professor suddenly burst into song. With a strange sense of arrogance, and terribly off-key, Chappy began to belt out a bizarre tune:

"Ol' mister stranger that nobody knows
He jingles and jangles where ever he goes."

It was very unlike the usually stoic professor to make light of such a desperate situation, once again proving how unstable he'd become and how far from grace he had fallen. Surely his solitary life had become his worst enemy. Chappy's hubris was short lived, however, and he suddenly felt sick to his stomach as he vomited in the dirt.

After the retching eased, the professor quickly collected the chain and keys from the dead body and easily rolled the slender man back over onto his back. In that process, the red bandana the pock-faced man wore around his forehead slipped down over his lifeless eyes. Suddenly his haunting stare stopped boring through Chappy's soul and the professor was grateful for the moment of peace.

The professor nimbly unbuckled the belt, and pulled it loose from the body as he dropped it in the dirt alongside of the bundle of keys. The pock-faced man wore a gold-capped tooth in the front of his mouth which glittered in the bright sunshine. For a long moment Chappy considered whether or not to retrieve the tooth until his better judgment took control.

Joe and Harry sniffed at the piled treasure with curiosity and then happily followed Chappy as he continued to move the corpse toward the slash pile and away from his home.

Without garbage service there tends to be a lot of trash that accumulates every day, even for one person. Naturally Chappy started a slash pile or burn pile right after he moved to Stillwater. He chose a secluded spot on his property in a fairly deep gully where the prevailing winds carried the smoke away from his cabin. He continually collected litter from around the wildlife refuge and always burned it with his personal trash from food packages, paper products, etcetera.

The burn pile was presently filled with old tree branches, cardboard boxes, and food containers that were waiting to become ash.

Chappy nonchalantly rolled the dead man's body down the incline onto the soft mound of trash. He added a few more branches on top of the corpse until it was fully covered, and then soaked the area with motorcycle gas. The fire lit quickly and burned hot as Chappy turned and walked away with Joe and Harry on his heels.

From that moment forward Doctor Morgan's pathetic and depleted soul suffered a relentless slide into the dark abyss. There would be no return from the depths of hell for this educated man. There would, however, be another day and more trash as he remained near the wildlife refuge for an additional forty years.

Chapter 25

As in most of small-town America, Fallon, Nevada had a gas station on nearly every corner in 1963. When Chappy drove his beautiful gold Avanti around town during the first days after his arrival he naturally received a lot of unwanted attention. He could not avoid the curious eyes, however, as he had business to conclude. Every young man pumping gas and working in the service garages took notice. It was hard to miss the tall blond man in the hot new sports car. The shiny new vehicle was a spectacular sight, and one that was seldom seen in rural communities. The Avanti became the topic of conversation in drug stores, gas stations, and coffee shops with no effort or permission from Charles Morgan. His mere arrival had set the local tongues to wagging.

The property Chappy purchased was located about forty miles from the heart of downtown along the same route one of the gas station attendants drove to his parents' home. Out of curiosity one afternoon, Ricky Jones followed Chappy to see where he and the gold Avanti were headed. As he watched from a safe distance behind, Ricky was astonished when Chappy turned into the long winding driveway of an old dilapidated cabin near the wildlife refuge. Ricky was disappointed, to say the least, and couldn't wait to share his new discovery with his friends. It was that very same evening when young Jones mentioned his secret to his new girlfriend who in turn shared the information with her dad while she worked the counter at the coffee shop. Her dad relayed some version of the tale to his co-workers the next morning at the truck stop near Reno and the dance was on!

The extraordinary sports car was a hot topic as was its owner who lived a few miles from the remote wildlife refuge. Young mechanics, known as *grease monkeys,* were impressed and inspired by the gold Avanti. Word spread like wildfire that a brand new one was being driven by a newcomer in Fallon, Nevada. There was lots more interesting chatter about the car and its owner especially after Chappy suddenly stopped driving the sports car all together.

The absence of the Avanti became the new topic of chatter and stimulated a multitude of theories about what had happened to it. It was that exact chatter that eventually reached the ears of some very bad men who had spent months searching for the illusive Professor Morgan. From Fallon to Reno and on to Sacramento, word traveled from one lip to another on every grease monkey intrigued with the story of the gold Avanti and the strange man who drove it.

At the same time, miles away from the high desert, the Studebaker dealership in San Francisco kept an especially lousy salesman on staff because Fredrick Winston had wanted him there. Winston held the papers on the car dealer's gambling debt. The salesman knew Chappy had bought a new gold Studebaker before leaving the city and he had mechanics on the payroll in several states report to him about every Avanti sighted. It wasn't too many more months before the gold Studebaker in Fallon, Nevada made it to the top of his list.

But then when Fredrick Winston died unexpectedly, his personal obsession with the gold Avanti died also. The gold sports car became totally unimportant to the dealership.

Studebaker went out of business and the lousy salesman, Moe Stackman was fired.

In the meantime, Chappy's attorney was desperate to locate his longtime friend. Through nefarious connections, Moe Stackman contacted Simon Pearle to make some fast money as the discreet private investigator Simon needed to hire to locate Chappy Morgan. By then Moe had a good idea of where Chappy was located and secretly intended to make the most of his lucky opportunity outside of the crime syndicate he was associated with. Simon Pearle had no idea whom he dealt with. During a night fueled with drugs, alcohol, and loose lips, Moe shared part of his plan with one of his gangster buddies, a Chinese man named Ho Chan Wang. The Asian wanted his share of the rich attorney's money that Moe had already been paid. He threatened Stackman with police intervention if Stackman didn't comply. Both men also knew that Professor Morgan was a very rich man and an easy mark.

When Stackman did not return with any cash and could not be located again, Ho Chan Wang was furious. He believed that Stackman had simply run off with the money and intended to leave Wang hanging high and dry and broke.

Eventually Wang also made his services available to Simon Pearle in the search for Chappy Morgan. He wanted the professor's great wealth for himself at any cost. As a member of a prominent Chinese crime family, Wang was both vicious and deceitful with an enormous chip on his shoulder that accompanied him into every room and caused a big ruckus with everyone around him. He considered himself to be a total badass when in reality he was nothing more than a two-bit hood. After imbibing in too much Saki, Ho Chan foolishly alerted another one of his mobster associates about his intention to become a very rich man upon his journey to Nevada. That mobster happened to be his boss and was known as Jangles. And Jangles did not take kindly to Wang's disrespect for *The Company* where his word was as good as Gospel.

Apparently these criminal characters who collectively targeted Charles Morgan's wealth could not keep their bravado in check. Loose lips placed each one of the swaggering imbeciles in jeopardy. Not even their inflated reputations were large enough to protect them against their own greed.

Although he may have been a heavyweight in the Chinese underground community, Ho Chan Wang was merely a puppet in the West Coast drug world where Jangles ran the show. The Asian owed Wilson Carver a small fortune in drug money which Carver intended to collect from him one way or the other. Thus, the clever pock-faced black man, known as Jangles, paid very close attention to the Asian's story about Chappy Morgan. After all, Wilson 'Jangles' Carver was the great puppet master.

Word of the tall blond man and his gold Avanti traveled quickly through the grapevine of teenage gossip in 1963 and unknowingly put Charles Morgan at great risk from several different men. Within several months, however, talk of the sports car migrated to other subjects and the reclusive professor was rarely, if ever, discussed again. In 1963, most of the lives in small-town America went on as usual except, of course, for its young soldiers and sailors who were headed to the shores of Viet Nam.

Chapter 26

To say that Professor Morgan existed meagerly is an understatement indeed. Although he enjoyed great success as a motivated and innovative scientist and was a rich man's son by birth, Chappy Morgan lived like a pauper in Nevada for more than forty years. His great wealth meant little to his new life near the Stillwater National Wildlife Refuge.

When he arrived in the Lahontan Valley in 1963 he purchased an entire section of land for cash which is equal to 640 acres. He made the purchase sight unseen and the land turned out to be wholly undeveloped.

Although a portion of his property once contained a large working junk yard, it was essentially abandoned years earlier by the previous owner. It currently resembles a rusted graveyard of badly wrecked automobiles with one perched on top of the other to about thirty-feet in height. The vehicles are mashed together with a couple of mistreated broken-down John Deer tractors and two rotted-out hay wagons along with various pieces of miscellaneous mining equipment. There are also four complete motorcycle skeletons hidden within the rusted steel fortress. But only one of them has been added since Morgan bought the place. A huge pyramid of used tires points toward the sky just inside the entry gate of his property. Considered by some to be an artistic sculpture, the black rubber tower stands guard over Chappy's entire acreage. Nevertheless, Morgan chose to live there where the remnants of the old high desert town of Stillwater, Nevada are nestled against the rugged mountains of the same name. He's grown to love the long morning shadows that sweep across the landscape. Chappy felt at home on the place instantly and cherished the privacy it has afforded. His land is the equivalent of one square mile of earth and is nothing but brush, alkali, a couple of sulfur springs, and an old broken-down homestead and junk yard.

If asked, no one would correctly guess why the brilliant man moved to the small Nevada farming community near the stagnant sink of the Carson River where he lives in a primitive old cabin with few modern conveniences. Why would an intelligent and educated man choose such a God-forsaken place where geothermal vents and hot springs dot the landscape and release obnoxious sulfur dioxide gas into the air?

Why deal with the alkali and mosquitoes and Great Basin Rattlesnakes? What kind of man would actually choose to live next to an abandoned junkyard? How could he want that life for himself?

Hardheaded and determined Chappy Morgan wanted exactly that and he has remained there in isolated glory for forty plus years with his huge assortment of books and journals and secrets. For all intents and purposes he became a hermit in spite of the fact that he was once a dazzling and handsome man with several degrees from Stanford University.

Although he spent his earlier years as a successful and prominent engineering professor, he inexplicably left his beloved San Francisco, The City by the Bay, shortly before his forty-fifth birthday never to return again to his former life. He liked being a solitary man with no interference.

Throughout the years, the professor has filled his days and nights with the study and examination of birds and insects.

He spent countless hours in the diverse wetlands near his dwelling where thousands of shorebirds pass through during their migration. He sighted and identified more than 280 species of birds in the area over the years and as a matter of course, he made impeccable drawings and kept detailed journals of each bird he encountered. As his passion for the wetlands grew, so did his collection of note books and loose papers leaving only a narrow trail navigable through the paper maze inside of his rustic abode. His insect collection boxes and jars filled with soil samples and rock pieces crowd every inch of open space not already covered by some sort of paper document. The old man has become a serious hoarder.

There are tin cans, milk cartons, and cardboard boxes crammed with Western trinkets and stashed in every nook and cranny around the old hermit's home. On a more curious note, one might notice with surprise that Chappy keeps a large bundle of Zig-Zag papers and several containers of loose tobacco on a small table beneath a beautiful handcrafted Tiffany stained-glass lamp. The object's beauty appears entirely out of character in his miserly residence and encourages the imagination to wander as to its benefactor and means of arrival there. There must be a lovely story to be heard about the Tiffany lamp, but Morgan is not talking. It is with deliberation and specific intention that there are very few, if any, visitors to his rundown cabin at the end of the long, narrow, and winding driveway. Charles Morgan simply does not like company. He's a loner and he wants to keep it that way.

The old codger's cabin is not unusual as the type of dwelling built during the early settlement of the West. Many shelters were built from a combination of clay soil and straw, called *adobe*. The wet materials were formed into bricks and set with a type of mortar for stability. What is quite unusual, however, is that the building itself was never modernized beyond the addition of electrical power and a partially completed septic sewer system in 1960. For all these years, Chappy has been forced to fill the toilet tank with buckets of water carried from the old-fashioned hand pump in his tiny kitchen. As a forty-five year old city boy, he adapted to the annoying procedure in spite of the difficulty. Thus, after forty years, the entire matter has become his normal routine rather than an inconvenience.

His cabin is constructed of heavy uneven timbers and adobe that is several inches thick. By design, the thick walls keep the rooms inside at a moderate and near constant temperature. The rough interior walls were finished by hand and Chappy whitewashed them only once in all the years he's lived there. So it is easy to understand why smoke and soot from decades of firewood burning inside his residence have left a dark film on the walls and ceiling of the small kitchen and across the large Wonder Stone fireplace in the main living area. Thick and sooty dust continually paints his window sills, bookshelves, and the sparse and dilapidated furniture throughout his house with a dark and inhospitable filth.

The white claw-footed bathtub, on the other hand, was never plumbed into the system. In the early days after his arrival, Chappy cut a hole in the bathroom floor and tried to jerry-rig a drain pipe that ran from the tub in the house outside to his vegetable garden. His intention was to kill two birds with one stone, so to speak, and use the same water twice. That idea only lasted until the first winter when the drain pipe froze solid for several weeks.

From then on bathing became much less important in the professor's life. Oh, there have been many times over the years when Charles Morgan dunked himself in the nearby reservoir, clothes and all, to rinse off the filth he accumulated. And there were also times during warm weather when he doused himself with the road department's high volume water pump. The long vertical hose that swung out from its steel frame was used to fill the county's large water trucks in order to manage dust control on the wildlife refuge. It offered Chappy a secret full-bodied shower. But he is required to sneak the water when the county trucks aren't in sight and only when he can manage to turn on the pump by himself. All things considered, clean water rarely touches the professor's body or his hair for many months at a time.

The old rascal remodeled the sod roof of his humble cabin at some point with the addition of several large sheets of corrugated tin. During Nevada's heavy winds, tin roofs have a tendency to rumble so Chappy threw a few tires on the metal roof to help stave off the irritating noise. The idea seemed like a good one at the time, if not an aesthetically pleasing one, but Mother Nature always manages to keep the upper hand. The old house is water tight during the summer thunderstorms and warm in the winter and that's all that ever mattered to the old professor.

His once sophisticated gold 1963 Studebaker Avanti with 240 horsepower from a V8 engine remains right where he parked it after his arrival in Stillwater. He apparently never turned the key again as the car's gold paint disintegrated in the harsh Nevada summers and bitter cold winters. After he broke out the Avanti's windows, squirrels and rats nested inside the beautiful car until its fine leather seats and expensive carpet are nearly unrecognizable. The classic car sits shamefully on its bare wheels because its tires were also added to the rubber collection on the roof of his cabin.

The once beautiful gold Avanti was only driven about two thousand miles before its demise.

Forty years' worth of scavenged miscellaneous junk collected from within the boundaries of his acreage as well as the desert surrounding his property has been arranged into mounds of waste. As he sees fit, he gradually adds his bits of precious junk to the rusted steel graveyard on his property. Anything the professor could carry by himself or haul in an old once-red Radio Flyer wagon has been added to his collection over the years.

Dangerous Intentions

The countless pieces of rusted steel create a huge and strange-looking sculptured wall that keeps a sullen and silent vigil over the area while serving as a self-styled fortress. No passerby can see beyond the rusted brown fortification into Chappy's private domain and that's just the way he designed it. Most every style and color of bottle that you can imagine forms a small glass mountain near the fortress. Irreverent and indestructible blades of salt grass protrude through broken shards of glass offering proof that life continues to thrive even in the most inhospitable of conditions, rather like Chappy Morgan his self.

The recluse's antique one-hole outhouse with its broken door hinges is a remnant from the earliest pioneer days in Stillwater. For all these years it has simply refused to fall down. As the outhouse leans precariously into his old tool shed, what remains of its door sways back and forth with the slightest breeze. The un-greased hinges provoke every listener with a ghostly sound as the wind in Nevada seems to blow every day.

After all these years that antique privy continues to keep the old man's secrets. The broken-down structure stands guard over Chappy's resident ghosts, rather like a ghost itself. It keeps company with a small bit of garden that is surrounded by the clutter of birdhouses, homemade whirly gigs, and clanging wind chimes. Neglected throughout the previous winter, the garden's soil has not yet been prepared for planting. But a couple of silent and tattered old scarecrows still keep vigil over Chappy's weedy and unattended yard. They are the ghosts' most constant companions.

Rustic wood planks attached by heavy iron hinges form the door of Chappy's large root cellar where apples, potatoes, and whatever else the garden produced are stored. It is dark and musty in the deep underground room providing the ultimate hiding place for a well-kept secret. Professor Morgan was very well-educated and very well versed on secrets too it seems.

He instinctively knew that every home needs a safe place to hide a good secret. This singular practice was not necessary, however, because the old recluse spread his secrets across the entirety of his property.

By contrast, the only semblance of real order and organization on the property is a wood pile located under a lean-to-shed about twenty-five feet from the old cabin. It houses cottonwood and oak logs precisely sized to fit the old man's cooking stove and rock fireplace. The logs are delivered and stacked every summer by one of Chappy's distant neighbors in the wood cutting business. Every summer the old man leaves the appropriate amount of wadded paper money plus an extra hundred dollar bill hidden in a rusty tobacco can nailed to a cottonwood stump. Every summer, just like clockwork, the heaping truck load of perfectly cut fire wood arrives without fanfare. It is placed under the protective eaves of the lean-to and neatly stacked in straight lines at just the right height for the old codger to easily pick up.

Only after the job is completely finished and the unnecessary wood chips are swept away, does the tobacco can turn up empty and back on the nail head waiting for the next year's delivery.

Chappy's wood pile is in need of replenishing.

Chapter 27

Charles Preston Morgan, a brilliant but curious man, is certainly an enigma. Once a well-dressed, distinguished, and handsome tall man with cobalt blue eyes and ruler straight posture, he's evolved into a caricature of his former self with stooped shoulders, a paunchy belly, and shuffling step. His thick yellow-white hair, once meticulously coiffed, is constantly tangled and hangs to the middle of his back in long matted ringlets. Whiskers and mustache cover his old face these days. And a beard hangs nearly to his naval with only his nose and gold rimmed glasses protruding from his cascading and messy locks. No one who ever knew the distinguished and gentle man from days gone by would recognize him now - even if they bumped into him on the sidewalk.

Over the course of forty plus years, Chappy has become unsightly at best. His body odor is unbearable for any civilized human to suffer because regular bathing is something that the professor left behind in California when he deserted the love of his life. There are no words to accurately describe how horribly he smells, he simply stinks to high heaven! His odor is intolerable.

This neglect is most apparent with the repulsive crusty dead skin cells that accumulate along the edge of his hairline, above his eyebrows, and around his neck and ears like the cradle cap of a newborn babe. He is an unbelievably disgusting human figure.

As incredible as it sounds, the old codger owns but a dozen pieces of clothing which he wears continuously regardless of the season. His bibbed overalls and long johns could probably stand in the corner by themselves if he ever took them off. But instead he works, eats, and sleeps in them every day of his life near the wildlife refuge. Each pair lasts several years and then when necessary the Sears catalog order arrives in Chappy's large mailbox by the side of the road. It is simply unnecessary for him to see anyone or to ever shop in the local stores in town.

His old fingernails are unbelievably long and strong, eerily so one might admit. Each and every nail is permanently stained from all that he has touched and studied during his forty-four years in Stillwater. Each one is at least an inch long and curves slightly inward toward the palm of his hand. Arthritis continues to distort his fingers in a most crippling and unkind manner.

With the slightest glance, it is apparent the old professor never bothers to brush his teeth or take care of his mouth at all. Forty-four years of rolling his own cigarettes have permanently stained his misshapen fingers and destroyed his few remaining snags of teeth. They have been left yellowed and unattractive, which adds to the foul smell and disgusting image the old man presents.

No one would ever guess those same hands once designed historically noble engineering achievements which improved the lives of people all over the globe. Nor would they believe those stained, unattractive, and neglected hands once held the elegant Caroline Righetti close to his heart and protected her with love and affection.

There is no evidence remaining on his person that suggests Chappy Morgan was ever anything more than a vagrant. His raggedy appearance is so thorough and complete that it contradicts the facts of his extensive education. It has become virtually impossible to recognize the dignified and well-respected scholar from the City by the Bay.

Charles Preston Morgan certainly made his own choices and lived his life on his own terms. But as surely as he created his solitary life he also transformed his soul in the high Nevada desert. Only his cobalt blue eyes, filled with the pain and sorrow of personal loss, offer a hint there might have been another time and another place for this lonely old man.

And it is positively true that the few words the old recluse spoke aloud near the stagnant sink of the Carson River were always articulated in a soft and breathy whisper and would have been totally unheard if the one who listened did not pay close and constant attention.

Chapter 28

Chappy Morgan died alone on a warm spring morning at the age of eighty-nine years as a large colony of American white pelicans arrived at the refuge. They were his favorite waterfowl with their huge vivid orange beaks nearly fourteen inches in length and a wingspan of nearly ten feet. He had been eager for their arrival after the particularly harsh winter subsided at his high desert home. His two partners, Joe and Harry waited several days beneath the barbed wire fence for his return. But the old man was never to walk with them again.

Wink Martin, the delivery man for the Green Thumb Grocery, used his key to unlock the main gate and drive into Chappy's rutted driveway alongside of the rusted wall of trash. He noticed that the old man was not waiting for him in his usual easy chair on the porch. Wink knew instantly that something was amiss because the old man had greeted the arrival of the delivery van in that exact spot every month for five years.

Chappy had a standing order on the first of every month with the Green Thumb for two gallons of milk, four loaves of bread, ten pounds of coffee, a large block of cheese, ten cans of sardines, two tins of Prince Albert tobacco, five pounds of ginger snap cookies, and the biggest jar of strawberry preserves

Dangerous Intentions

the store carried, and the largest package of toilet tissue too. Once in a while as a special treat he added Hershey chocolate bars, saltine crackers, and ripe bananas to the list. But usually his order remained exactly the same.

He always paid in cash and always gave Wink a twenty dollar tip. It had been the same every month for five years. And Wink looked forward to seeing the old crusty character even though they never shared more than a word or two. It was a familiar routine that both men seemed comfortable with.

Cautiously, Wink entered the old man's home after he first knocked and yelled for the eccentric old codger. He felt a bit nervous about what he might find. As he made his way through the six-foot-high maze of boxes, books, and notebooks into the small room at the end of the hall, he could see the old man lying in quiet repose. Wink thought the man looked blissful and content. It was as if he was in dreamlike state with his long silver beard lying across his chest. His matted yellow-white mange of hair was spread out around his head on the dark stained pillow and bare mattress. His gold rimmed glasses were carefully placed on a stack of newspapers beside his rickety narrow single bed and he was fully clothed. A hand-rolled cigarette appeared as little more than a long grey ash on the old saucer next to his bed. Worn out lace-up boots waited for Chappy alongside the notebook and pencil set he prepared to use that morning to sketch the white pelicans.

Wink called out to the old man once again in case he was deep in sleep. "Mr. Morgan," he stated flatly with hesitation. "Mr. Morgan, are you alright?"

When there was no response he touched the professor's neck to check for a pulse. There wasn't one. Chappy's reclusive days had come to an end.

Charles Morgan did not have a telephone so Wink used his own cell phone to call the sheriff as he looked around at the amazing den the brilliant but strange man called home.

It was his first time inside the old codger's place and he was overwhelmed by the accumulation of clutter and total lack of cleanliness. There was no radio, no television, and not a single electrical appliance in sight that Wink could see. Bare light bulbs with filthy pull-strings gave the dark and austere rooms a burst of clinical white glare. Only a single delicate stained- glass lamp provided a hint of hominess to the otherwise depressing place.

A mouse scampered across Wink's path which caused him to shudder at the realization of the disgusting and unthinkable conditions Chappy Morgan had created for his solitary life on the 640 acres of salt grass and alkali.

He had never seen anything remotely like the professor's abode and figured he never would again as he wandered back through the maze and into the warm spring sunshine to wait for the sheriff and the coroner.

Chapter 29

Young Martin was sitting in the old codger's rocking chair on the front porch listening to a wind chime made from a collection of keys and chain links when the sheriff arrived. The chime, directly over the front door of the cabin, jingled in the breeze and gave Wink an incredibly weird sensation. He was caught off-guard by the uneasy feeling and even felt a bit nauseous. He noted that the tall wooden rocking chair was oddly decorated with a leather belt nailed diagonally across the back of the rocker. The belt was worn smooth from use but the engraved name of *Jangles* was still vaguely legible as Wink ran his fingers over the leather. Something about the feel of it made him suddenly uncomfortable as a cold chill swept through his body. He remembered someone called Jangles from his distant past….but surely it couldn't be the same man?

Wink was mulling things over in his mind about the man called Jangles as well as the reclusive Mr. Morgan whom he had known for five years. He felt that it was a strange and bizarre life the brilliant man designed for himself in such an unholy place when a whole world of opportunities lay at his feet.

Obviously the old codger had plenty of money that came from somewhere because Wink knew the old man never worked at a regular job. At least that's what he had heard from his friends at the Green Thumb Grocery. Wink pondered the reasons why Chappy dropped out of his own life to live in such desolate surroundings with barely the basic needs of civilization. It was a quandary indeed.

"Howdy, Sheriff," Wink called out as the tall man in uniform approached. "He's inside in the bedroom at the end of the hall. I haven't touched anything except the old man himself to see if he was breathing. He was cold to the touch so I guess he's been gone a while. I'm not sure you can get a gurney in there now because it's a pretty amazing place. I've never seen so much stuff piled up in one house before. He wasn't much of a housekeeper."

"Thanks for calling this in. We'll get him to the mortuary as soon as possible and then we need to have a look around. Did you know much about Mr. Morgan?"

"No Sir, Sheriff," Wink stated quickly, "He was a real private individual. I've been delivering his groceries and supplies every month for about five years now and I can't say that I even had a conversation with the man."

"He just gave me a list of the stuff he wanted and always paid me with cash. He was a generous guy though and he gave me a twenty dollar tip every time."

"Just look at that car, Sheriff, it's a classic," Wink added, waving his hand toward the parked automobile. "I think it's a Studebaker Avanti with a V8 engine. About 1963 I'd guess. What would that be worth today if it hadn't been left here to rot? What would possess a guy to let something like that happen to such a beautiful classic car?"

"I don't know, Wink; I find it difficult to guess what drives people to do the things they do."

The sheriff and Wink casually walked over to inspect the old Avanti and the two men briefly looked inside the car for any identification that might be left.

Disappointed, the sheriff continued.

"Looks like the old boy tore the vehicle identification number (VIN) out a long time ago and there are no plates on this rig. That's going to complicate things for us to find any information about his next of kin. Let's get inside the house and see what we've got to work with."

Wink once again accompanied the sheriff into the rustic old cabin. Upon entering the sheriff exclaimed, "You were right about the gurney, Wink. We'll have to clear some of this clutter out of the way. Would you mind helping me and the boys move some of these boxes and books? We can make quicker work of getting him out of here that way."

"Sure thing, Sheriff," Wink agreed. "I'd be glad to help. What's going to happen to all this stuff?" he asked as he hoisted several boxes out of the hallway and placed them in the kitchen. "Someone really needs to go through all these books and drawings, looks like there are hundreds of them."

"But there are no photographs, Wink," the sheriff added. "I find that real strange. Most homes have photographs and various memorabilia out in plain view. But then, maybe this beautiful lamp was the only memory he cared to look at. You just never know about some folks."

The sheriff continued with authority. "I did some checking on him after you called this in, Wink, and there hasn't been much of a paper trail on Mr. Morgan since he bought this place in 1963. He kept a real low profile and paid his taxes way in advance with cash when he moved in here. The old man's history here in the valley is a bit hazy, to say the least."

"He apparently used several different names along the way and there's no clear and precise record of just who he is. This address still has a credit on the books at the power company even after forty years. In my estimation, that took a pretty good chunk of change to start out with. He's been a mighty private fellow for a long time now which adds to the mystery for certain."

"Our Mr. Morgan never applied for a Nevada driver's license or purchased a vehicle in the state that I could find. That Studebaker outside appears to have been his last vehicle and since it doesn't have tags on it and Studebaker has been out of production for more than forty years, it will be pretty tough for us to pick up a lead regarding his purchase. We can find the VIN number stamped on the frame rail with a little effort. But that situation pretty much leads us to a complete dead end regarding his automobile, and that, my young friend, certainly doesn't happen very often I must say."

As the sheriff moved the last of the boxes obstructing the gurney he added, "I'll venture a guess that our Mr. Morgan wasn't interested in being found, Wink. This day and age that's a pretty tall order simply because of technology. It has become very difficult to live below the radar, so to speak. People know about one another and find out about their secrets. It's just amazing that someone could reside here in the county for more than forty years and have so little known about him."

"Yes, Sir, that's a fact." Wink said emphatically.

"He must have spent a lot of time watching the birds and bugs to fill up this many books. I'm kind of sorry now that I never talked to him about all this stuff because he would have been real interesting to talk with. He just didn't seem the type for conversation, being so private and kind of strange."

"He just kept to himself in this old broken-down cabin and walked everywhere he went. I heard Toby Howard took him to town once to get a tooth pulled and buy stamps, but even that was years ago."

"Well, Wink, that about does it for now," the sheriff stated as he dusted off his uniform.

"We're going to fence off this property and put up some law enforcement signs to keep out the looky-loos that are bound to show up once word of his death spreads around town." The sheriff paused to look around and then continued.

Dangerous Intentions

"I'm going to assign a deputy to investigate the place until we can figure out who has authority over it. Thanks for your help, Son, I appreciate it very much."

"You bet, Sheriff," Wink affirmed. "I need to get all these groceries back to the store. Mr. Morgan certainly won't need them anymore."

Chapter 30

Wink Martin had recently celebrated his twenty-second birthday with his friends at the race track where he lives in a small travel trailer behind the stables. His arrival in town five years earlier, on the day of his seventeenth birthday, was a brutal awakening for the young man as he was rousted off the Union Pacific train. He and his few belongings were dumped like trash near the livestock yard not far from the railroad siding. Luckily he was not detained by railroad officials and the stash of marijuana and cocaine in his duffle bag remained undiscovered.

Still high from his last hit, Wink mindlessly stumbled into the empty fairgrounds nearby where two hefty and homeless drifters assaulted him. They stole his duffle and the cash in his trouser pockets and then left him unconscious and bleeding inside the men's restroom. When he was found later by the off-duty janitor he was taken to the first-aid station where Jesse Garcia patched him up and hauled him into the small travel trailer to rest. Jesse saw something in the young man's eyes that kept him from calling the police and turning the teenaged stranger over to the authorities.

It was something that Wink would be grateful for as the days and weeks ahead turned into the rest of his life.

Jesse Garcia took a personal interest in Wink and nursed him carefully back to health with the loving help of his tiny wife, Elena. The first few days were difficult ones as the young addict suffered the effects of serious cocaine withdrawal. He wretched and heaved with cold sweats and chills as Jesse held him close and reassured him that the days ahead would soon be better ones. The teenager hallucinated during fitful periods of sleep and acted out against Jesse with violence and vulgar words but the kind hearted Hispanic man never gave up nursing the young stranger back to good health.

As the worst symptoms began to ease for Wink Martin, Jesse began to feed the boy warm nutritious Mexican soups and Elena's handmade tacos and enchiladas. The boy's strength was slowly restored and his eyes and complexion cleared. Wink Martin was freed of the demon drugs.

Jesse put the young stranger to work as soon as he was able to support his own weight and there were no questions asked as he began to care for the horses that were stabled near the racetrack. Elena provided him with clothes and boots as Wink became another accepted member of the large family of workers Jesse supervised.

The teenager quickly discovered a fondness for the large animals and soaked up every bit of knowledge about horses and racing that Jesse could share with him. He cleaned the stalls, bucked hay bales, shoveled manure, and learned to groom the horses with care and respect as they were exercised and trained to race. Wink felt right at home with Jesse, Elena, and the rest of the working men who were happy to let him be himself. With no further need to impress anyone or to hide from anything in his life, and with thanks for Jesse's help, Wink no longer lusted after drugs and alcohol. He was at peace for the first time that he could remember in his seventeen years.

Wink Martin started driving part-time for the Green Thumb Grocery a few weeks after Jesse introduced him to the owner.

He liked both employers very much and kept himself busy by taking some evening classes at the community college after his mornings working with the horses and afternoons driving the Green Thumb delivery van. Wink was very much at ease in the small Nevada town where he landed totally by accident. And Jesse was very pleased with his decision to guide Wink out of harm's way. It worked out well for both men and had been the right thing to do.

Chapter 31

After weeks of searching for answers about Chappy Morgan, the deputy in charge of the investigation had found very little information. Toni Canon had been with the sheriff's department about five years and she had never been more frustrated with an investigation. There were no clues as to the old man's family history or any information about where he may have lived prior to his arrival in Stillwater, Nevada. He kept no bank accounts or insurance policies and never attended any church or social organization that the deputy was able to discover. Very few people, other than the folks at the Green Thumb Grocery and Toby Howard, the wood cutter, had even heard his name mentioned before.

As daylight was turning to dusk, Toni decided to investigate the old codger's root cellar which had not been searched since the investigation began. She struggled to get the heavy wood door open and discovered the entrance was covered in thick dusty cobwebs.

Using a broom she cautiously cleared her way into the dark and musty recess under the earth. The dimming shaft of light from the large open door eerily highlighted the dusty air.

Toni proceeded cautiously into the underground cavern with only her flashlight and a broom for assistance. The cellar was cluttered with stacks of stuff much like the old timer's house. There were barrels and buckets filled with rotten apples, pears, and apricots. Some soggy potatoes, limp radishes and rotted turnips stunk up one corner of the stuffy room. And there were piles of carrots still attached to their long fern-like green tops in a big heap on the cool earthen floor.

The deputy found a large collection of Ball wide-mouth canning jars lined up on a shelf in the underground room as she moved carefully across the near-dark chamber to view them. One of the jars contained individual animal teeth of various sizes. One was filled nearly to the top with rattlesnake rattles and buttons and another with snake skins coiled tightly inside. Another of the jars contained pieces of turquoise rock and yet another was filled with magnificent arrowheads.

Upon closer inspection, Toni realized one of the larger jars on the far left and back of the shelf was actually an old goldfish bowl. Stepping closer, with her flashlight focused directly on the glass vessel, she could see an object nestled inside the dusty round cavity. As she awkwardly lifted the bowl from its hiding place with one hand, a small mouse suddenly darted across the wood shelf only inches from her face. The rodent's movement startled the deputy so badly that she nearly dropped her flashlight and broom as well as the bowl balanced in her hands as she jerked back from the tiny creature.

Toni Canon unexpectedly felt spooked in the musty cellar. She knew it was foolish, but she spoke out loud to calm herself with the sound of her own voice. "Canon, get a hold of yourself. You know there's no one else down here but you."

As she collected her thoughts and regained her composure, Toni cautiously squatted on the earthen floor with the glass bowl perched on one knee. With the flashlight held securely in one hand, she reached into the dusty container with the other and lifted an object tightly wound in very old newspaper. As she began to un-wrap the hidden item, the newspaper wrapping began to crumble in her hands. Inside she found an authentic looking miniature cable car inscribed along both sides with flaking white paint. It read: *San Francisco Wharf.* Toni whispered, "Finally a real clue, you old rascal."

While inspecting the souvenir, the deputy was surprised once again as a large coin suddenly fell out of the miniature cable car and jingled back into the dusty goldfish bowl. Retrieving the coin, Toni recognized it as an 1878 Morgan silver dollar minted in Carson City, Nevada. Deputy Canon found the solitary hidden treasure to be somewhat out of place in the underground earthen room filled with decaying fruits and vegetables. But she also found it to be incredibly interesting. It seemed to be the only thing of value in the dark cellar and the only visible clue that might lead to the identity of the old man's family. Deep in thought about this surprising new evidence, she returned the silver coin and the cable car souvenir to the safety of the glass bowl which she then tucked under one arm and carried with her as she examined the rest of the underground cavern.

There were broken-down wooden fruit boxes in many sizes and shapes that were filled to overflowing with newspapers and journals. Hordes of them it seemed to the deputy as she carefully made her way through the stacks, stumbling slightly along the way. Bundles of blankets and remnants of old carpet and miscellaneous pieces of cloth fabric were tied together and stacked nearly to the ceiling in one section of the root cellar. Thick choking dust boiled out of the bundles as Toni whacked them with the broom in utter disbelief as she passed by.

After a sneezing fit from thumping the dusty bundles with the broom, the deputy was drawn cautiously toward a large mound of burlap that appeared to be tied with some type of rope or twine. Pausing for a moment to retrieve her handkerchief and wipe her dripping nose, she set the goldfish bowl and flashlight down on the mound of burlap. As she wiped her nose, Toni nonchalantly kicked at the mound with a lawman's curiosity. To her complete surprise, the rotted old twine simply gave way in the near darkness and something rolled out of the pile with a soft thud onto the earthen floor.

Grabbing the flashlight, the cautious young deputy shone the light at her feet and was completely unprepared for her unexpected discovery. A human skull lay at her feet only inches from the burlap bundle she'd just kicked. Toni Canon gasped and then quickly clasped her handkerchief across her mouth. Gathering her thoughts she asked aloud, "Oh my God, Mr. Morgan, what have you done?"

Stunned by her discovery and not certain of her surroundings, Toni turned her body slowly in a complete circle shining the light around the underground room. In the far corner, her flashlight suddenly reflected off something shiny in the darkness which caught her attention. With her knees feeling weak and shaky she barely distinguished the outline of a lidded box covered with dirt and leaves. As she made her way closer she swept the bulk of debris off the box to discover a small antique round-top trunk. It was securely fastened with leather straps and several ornate silver buckles.

The deputy held her breath for a moment as she dragged the heavy old trunk to a more open area of the cellar where there was ample room to open it. She was naturally worried about what else she might find hidden in the secret room. Toni approached the trunk with extreme caution.

Luckily the trunk was not locked and as Toni Canon unbuckled the black leather straps and lifted the lid she was totally amazed by its contents. Hidden in the round-top trunk was nothing but U. S. currency. The trunk was filled with loose bills in denominations from one dollar to one-hundred dollars as well as hundreds of shiny quarters. Toni could not believe her eyes as she ran her fingers through the piles of money in the spot light of the simple flashlight. "Holy shit, would you look at this!" she exclaimed privately.

"Sheriff, you need to get out here as soon as possible," the young deputy said, speaking as calmly as possible into the police radio. "Bring some lights. You're not going to believe what I just found out here at Morgan's place."

Chapter 32

Toni Canon, the middle child born in a family of five children, was always an intelligent, pampered and beautiful girl with blue-green eyes and long dark curly hair. Named Antoinette Becca Canon, in honor of her great grandmother, she absolutely hated the ultra-feminine role her mother chose for her. Antoinette preferred to be called Toni from the time she was a toddler. Her strong will and independent spirit proved to be a serious challenge for both her parents, but most especially for her quiet petite mother who was totally infatuated with social status.

Antoinette intensely disliked the fussing and primping that took place behind closed doors when she wanted to be climbing trees and chasing after her four brothers instead. She loathed the frilly designer dresses made of ruffled satins and fine silks that her mother forced her to wear. And her pretty polished toes always felt pinched in the awkward little high-heeled slippers that matched each outfit perfectly.

Eliza Canon fondly referred to her beautiful daughter as *my little princess*, and just hearing those words made Toni cringe.

The eldest child of the Canon family was Antoinette's brother, Andrew Baxter Canon. He was four years older than she and especially fond of his little sister. They were kindred spirits, so to speak, and shared their deepest secrets with one another. He often called his only sister *Alfie,* a special pet name he gave her as soon as she was old enough to realize that the five Canon kids' initials were *ABC.* With wonderment one morning, Toni announced that they were the *alphabet kids* and Andrew howled with laughter and swung her around the room in circles like a merry-go-round. It was a silly thing really, and so simple. But the name Alfie meant the world to Antoinette.

Those few treasured moments from her childhood were meant to last her a lifetime. Andrew always made Toni feel very, very special. She was bonded to her favorite brother forever. Over the years, Andrew kept a watchful eye on Toni and protected her from any trouble that came her way, which often times included Alex Barlow Canon, her brother just two years older than she. Alex was a constant pest and trouble maker. He teased everyone in the family and often provoked sibling rivalries between the two younger brothers, Adrian Burton and Aaron Beck. There was never a dull moment in the busy Canon household.

While she was a young child, it was compulsory for Antoinette to attend ballet lessons every week where she achieved great success in spite of her tomboy attitudes. She was very agile and athletically inclined and moved rather quickly into the advanced classes which thrilled her proud mother. Her music lessons, however, did not go nearly so well. From the beginning Toni hated playing the violin with a passion felt deep in her soul.

It was the one instrument her mother insisted she learn to play. Poor Toni always had a stomach ache of some sort or a throbbing headache or a sore knee when she arrived at the music studio. It was like pulling teeth to merely get her in the door. The instructor suffered extreme frustration for months on end as Antoinette deliberately made her violin screech and howl throughout the lessons.

After nearly driving her mother, as well as her music teacher mad with her antics, Antoinette finally won the battle against the violin and was allowed to switch to piano lessons which she enjoyed much more.

As Toni grew older she suffered through long tedious tennis lessons and modeling classes along with intense instruction for cotillion instead of the karate and pistol range practice she secretly longed for. Her four brothers were allowed to do all the things that Toni coveted for herself. She felt that being treated like a feminine girly girl was totally unfair.

By the time Antoinette was thirteen years old she developed into a gorgeous young woman with an outspoken mind of her own. It wasn't in Toni's nature to sugar coat anything about her life. She simply called things as she saw them no matter how impolite she seemed. On the night of a dinner party her mother arranged, Antoinette Canon cut off her own beautiful long dark hair in the secrecy of her bedroom. She arrived at the family dinner table wearing a cute pixie-style haircut and an enormous smile which nearly sent her mother to the emergency room in shocked disbelief.

Savvy thirteen year old Antoinette Becca Canon found her own voice that day and made her wishes known in front of the entire family and their sophisticated guests. And she did it on her own terms. From that day forward she happily and successfully chose her own path.

There were no more ballet lessons or modeling classes and certainly no more afternoon teas with her mother's hoity-toity friends. Antoinette Becca Canon was free at last to become the woman she wanted to be. She simply became Toni Canon. Her dreams blossomed and her spirits soared.

But Toni's life was suddenly thrown into a tail spin and virtually ground to a halt on the night after her eighteenth birthday when her beloved brother, Andrew, was killed by a drunk driver. Twenty-two year old Andrew Baxter Canon, the love of her life, was returning to the University of Nevada in

Dangerous Intentions

Reno after Toni's birthday party when a Ford pickup barreled through the red light near his apartment complex and broadsided Andrew's sports car. Andrew never knew what hit him. Toni, however, certainly knew what hit her and she toppled like a stack of bricks.

The entire family was suddenly thrust into deep mourning for their beloved son and brother. Each of the Canons struggled with their own profound and personal grief to the total exclusion of one another. Twenty-year-old Alex immediately attempted to drown his sorrows with Jack Daniels Whiskey. He nearly drank himself to death in the process while Toni's dad, Oliver Canon, buried himself at work for weeks on end. Oliver's grief led him carelessly into several brief and meaningless affairs with young assistants from his law firm as he was deeply entrenched in his own denial.

It was grace alone that saved Oliver Canon as he finally extended a father's hand and a humbled heart to young Alex just when his troubled son needed him most. Together father and son found their way through tears and grief to a safe harbor of peaceful sanity, sobriety, and the rest of their sorrow-filled family. Toni's twin brothers, Adrian and Aaron threw themselves into their athletic pursuits at the local high school and managed to keep themselves totally exhausted and numbed to the emotions that engulfed their lives. They became focused, dedicated, formidable opponents which was something that served them well into the future. Toni, however, kept a watchful eye on them from a distance as she waited and worried about the emotional cracks that were sure to engulf her younger twin brothers. But the cracks had not yet openly appeared.

Sadly, it was Toni's mother, Eliza Canon, who lost touch with reality for long periods of time and nearly lost herself along the way. She discovered an offbeat religion and immersed her soul in the Word of God as seen through the eyes of a previously outcast preacher who had strayed from his own flock. He absconded with the tithes and offerings and engaged in inappropriate sexual escapades with the young women of his congregation. He was also an ex-felon which Eliza did not know at the time. His charismatic nature persuaded the grieving mother of his good intentions when in fact he preyed upon her emotional distress with misguided counsel and sticky fingers in her wallet.

Strict, rigid beliefs consumed every facet of Eliza's life as she neglected her husband and children for many months. She was totally lost within herself and sought answers that she was unable to find even with her preacher. As Oliver Canon began to pay better attention to his wife, he also began to unravel the truth about her promiscuous preacher. The district attorney eventually intervened and removed the self-described prophet from the scene with criminal charges once again.

Eliza ultimately relinquished her obsession with her social status in the community as she continued to search for answers in the Scriptures and Bible stories. Through several community outreach programs she was able to redirect her abundant energy and strong faith in a more positive manner which miraculously led her back to her family. Eliza Canon gave countless hours of her time to the community's poor children as well as the downtrodden older souls of town. Not to mention the countless dollars of her husband's wealth that generously found their way into the offering plates.

Eighteen year old Antoinette Canon turned her grief inward with the loss of her beloved brother. She suffered alone in silence questioning her own faith and her own purpose in life. She was a lost little lamb with no hope in sight. Her entrance into college was delayed while she struggled to regain her balance and composure. She spent hours and hours wearing Andrew's favorite shirt because she wanted to keep the smell of him close to her always. Toni was afraid she would lose her brother completely if she took the shirt off or laundered it like her mother demanded.

The young woman listened to her brother's favorite music for hours on end until it was imprinted on her being and then his music became her own. At times it was difficult to know if it was her life or Andrew's that she was trapped in. Toni simply could not find her way out of the dark and deep hole she had tumbled into.

Antoinette couldn't spend time with her friends because she couldn't bear to see them happy or to listen to their laughter. No one understood her. Everyone thought they could help her, but no one could. Everywhere she looked she saw Andrew. If only she could speak to him one more time, there were so many things she wanted to say to him. She was literally sick with grief, and it seemed there was no end in sight to her loneliness. Toni barely ate enough to keep a small bird alive and slept only for a few stolen moments at a time when her thoughts of Andrew grew calm.

Months went by before Toni felt like she could actually breathe again without weeping, without thinking of Andrew every minute of every single day and every night. Weeks of counseling and hours of writing in her journal helped lift the heavy cloud that nearly smothered her spirit. And then suddenly, without warning one bright and sunny morning, Toni opened her heart to a brand new day. With clear eyes and a quieted soul, she reflected on the gift that Andrew had given her on her eighteenth birthday. As a warm feeling of peace and acceptance washed over her like a warm generous hug from an old friend, she realized that her brother had left her with a legacy of love and a heart full of warm loving memories. She was finally ready to move forward.

Toni gently held the delicate gold necklace that Andrew had given her for her eighteenth birthday. As she opened the small locket, she wiped away the last of her tears and finally smiled easily. She softly whispered "Alfie" as she ran her fingers across the locket. Just that one single word was engraved on the gold heart-shaped locket and it meant the world to Toni. Smiling, she fondly remembered the day her brother had first called her by that name. She knew her nick- name was a thoughtful treasure that Andrew had given her and it was far more precious than any jewel. It was something special meant just for her when she was such a little girl. The name was a wonderful gift, one that Toni would always treasure. It was the one solitary moment in their lives that no one else could share. It belonged to Alfie and Andrew.

Toni's nickname was engraved in beautiful script lettering on the front side of the gold heart-shaped locket beneath a spray of tiny roses. She slowly whispered the words written inside the locket. "The future is yours – go get it! Love, Andrew."

Toni closed the locket, lifted it gently to her lips and kissed it ever so sweetly. She then placed the gold chain and locket around her neck. "I will Andrew, but I'll miss you." she whispered. "Thank you so much. I love you."

Chapter 33

Four million six hundred thousand and eighty-three dollars were taken from the trunk in Chappy's root cellar, along with one 1878 Morgan Carson City silver dollar that was estimated to be worth several thousand dollars in the coin collecting world. It was more cash than anyone in town had ever seen in one place at one time. Unfortunately there were no distinguishing marks to identify where it had come from. The Federal Depository could not give any additional information about the various serial numbers other than the fact that the money had come from their western division. The Bank of the West accepted the large amount of cash to keep in their vault until proper ownership was determined.

The small-town local media was suddenly interested in the death of the reclusive millionaire and it became a difficult task to keep them off of the old codger's property and out of his house.

Without his personal identification papers available such as a driver's license or social security card, there was serious confusion about exactly who Chappy really was. No one, it seemed, appeared to know the slightest thing about the old man or his history. The sheriff relied on the Green Thumb Grocery store to be one of the most reliable sources he could find as they had done business with the secretive man for several decades and knew his name to be Charles Morgan.

Various county records as well as the local utility company listed several versions of his name which only added more confusion to the matter. One record listed him as Morgan Preston on the entry and as Preston Charles on a different page. Another gave his name as M. P. Chapman and the recorder's office listed the property to Preston Morganchap aka C. P. Morgan. Whether it was deliberate deception by the owner or handwritten errors made by entry-level employees remained uncertain. Whatever the reason, it caused the sheriff great consternation.

Tipsters and phony family members came out of the woodwork to lay claim to the newly discovered millions which greatly complicated the search for genuine next of kin. Frustrated by the media frenzy, the sheriff hired a second taller chain link and barbed wire fence built to protect the entire property and the contents of the eccentric professor's home. A higher priority was assigned to the case and Deputy Canon was given the green light to increase the investigation and bring it to a speedier conclusion.

After a class on forensic psychology where Toni Canon was a guest speaker, Wink Martin introduced himself to the young attractive deputy. He told her of his deliveries to the Morgan property, finding the old man dead, and his discussion with the sheriff about the curious nature of Chappy's life. He asked the deputy if there was any way he might assist her in the search for the old recluse's next of kin as a part of his studies in forensic psychology and she assured him that she would run it by the sheriff and get back to him.

That conversation had taken place weeks earlier and Wink had been assisting Deputy Canon with the investigation ever since.

As the days turned into weeks, Wink Martin and Toni Canon examined more and more of Chappy's notebooks and

Dangerous Intentions

journals hoping to discover some clues that would lead them to the man's next of kin. They continued with the search without much success until they finally located a personal pencil sketch hidden in his book entitled *Egrets and Gulls*.

The sketch was of a particularly frail looking woman in a large rocking chair. She had little emotion, if any on her face. Her eyes were deep set and hollowed and there were dark shadows under her eyes. Her long hair hung in a single braid on one side of her head and she held a Bible in her lap. There was no inscription on the picture and Toni and Wink both found the sketch to be haunting and quite unsettling. It was the closest thing to a picture of death that either of them could imagine.

The second sketch, in the back of another notebook entitled *Cinnamon Teal,* was found later that same week. It was a lovely drawing of a young beautiful ballerina. She was dressed in a tutu, poised on pointed toe with arms gracefully bent overhead. Toni recognized the ballet position as one she had struggled with as a young ballerina years earlier during her dance lessons. The child in the drawing was smiling and her eyes were bright with youth and anticipation. It was a much happier scene than the previous sketch the couple had found. The words *Merry little Mary* were inscribed across the bottom of the drawing next to a second pair of delicately drawn ballet slippers with their ribbon laces trailing off the edge of the paper.

"Who were you, Charles Morgan and why did you live here like this for so many years?" Toni inquired aloud. She was desperate to find the answers.

Chapter 34

The young deputy and her assistant easily became friends during their long and frustrating search through the contents of Chappy's house. Toni was six or seven years older than Wink and she was surprised by that fact because Wink seemed old beyond his years. During the course of their investigation they shared an emotional bond based on mutual respect and the intense nature of searching Chappy's most personal items. After the first of the old codger's personal sketches were found, their conversations naturally took a more private direction as Toni inquired about Wink's past.

"Where did you live before you moved to our little slice of heaven, Wink?" she asked as they moved several more boxes nearer the table where they were examining the contents.

"Oh, I've lived in a lot of places," he replied nonchalantly. "I sort of moved around a lot when I was a kid. But there's really no place but Fallon that I've called home for very long. I was born near Portofino, Italy but I was only there a couple of years so I don't remember anything about it. My mother was sort of a hippie and a gypsy and we moved to several cities in Italy for about ten years before we came to the United States."

"Really?" She questioned, surprised by his answer. "What an exotic life you've had. That's quite an adventure compared to mine. I was born here and have lived here all my life except while I was away at college and then at the police academy. I always said I would leave and see the world, but here I am still in the same small town."

"I think it's great that you have such strong ties to your home and family." Wink said with a hint of nostalgia. "I guess that's the one thing I would change about my life if I could."

"My family is ok," Toni said with a sigh. "Not perfect by any means, but they are still my family. Sometimes family is just not all that it's cracked up to be."

"That sounds a little ominous, Deputy."

"Well, you sound a little melancholy yourself," Toni said with concern as she opened another box of Chappy's journals. "Wink, what about your family; aren't they here with you?"

"No, I haven't seen my family for a long time. I don't remember my dad and things didn't go too well between my mom and me, so I've pretty much been on my own for a while now. Jesse and Elena Garcia are the closest to family that I have. Do you know them?"

Toni Canon was glad their conversation turned to a happier subject. She could tell by the look on Wink Martin's face that he was sensitive about discussing his past and she felt that she had said more about her own life than she intended to.

"Yes, I do actually," the deputy responded happily. "They are lovely people and Elena is a wonderful cook. You're really lucky if she cooks for you, Wink! She has catered a couple of parties that I've been to and her food is amazing.

Jesse has helped with our equestrian unit teaching safety techniques. I think you're in good hands with them."

Pausing a moment, she added, "I don't mean to pry, Wink, but sometimes it helps to talk about the things that are bothering us and get things out in the open. If you ever want to talk I'm here to listen."

"Deputy, are you interrogating me?"

Martin teased Toni with a wink as he carried another box of books to the completed pile. "Maybe I'll tell you my story sometime," he added with a sigh, "But not here, and not with any people around. There's stuff I'm not too proud of and I'd hate to have you kick me out of here because of it."

"Well, I don't think that's likely to happen, the deputy said laughing, "So if you ever want to talk, just let me know and I'll leave my badge in the car."

"Okay," Martin winked. "You've got a deal, Deputy, but only if you tell me something about your life too!"

Toni and Wink searched through many more journals filled with drawings of birds and insects when the deputy finally came upon another of Chappy's personal pencil sketches. It was an extremely odd picture and one that Toni could not quite understand in lieu of the others they had found. The sketch was merely of a block of letters and numbers outlined with a heavy bold stroke. It read: 5KGQ436.

"What do you make of this, Wink," the officer asked?

"I'm not sure," he replied. "Do you think it's a code of some sort, maybe the combination for a safe or a safe deposit box? But then you know, Toni, it looks like it could be a license plate number."

"Good guess, Wink. I think that's exactly what this is. Good job! We'll be saving this one too. I'm sure the sheriff will be interested in this."

Later, in a book labeled *White-faced Ibis*, Toni Canon found another particularly personal and sentimental drawing.

It was a lovely picture of a beautiful young woman with a rugged coastal view in the background. Toni suddenly felt as if she were looking into Chappy Morgan's soul, somehow invading his privacy. It made her quietly uncomfortable.

In the drawing, the featured woman looked to be tall and thin with huge expressive eyes and long dark hair cascading below her shoulders. She was smiling slightly as she stood on the bluff near a wind-swept tree holding a bouquet of flowers with her back to the sea. The picture was simply inscribed with *222 Sea Mist Drive*. Wink took the sketch from Toni and held the picture for a long time staring at the woman's face as if he were memorizing the scene. Deputy Canon's attention was drawn to his pensive expression as the two sat in silence for an extended period of time. As she returned her focus upon the search, Toni suddenly distracted him as she directed his attention to yet another new find.

Inside of another cardboard box, Toni found a four inch square hand-carved wooden box with a similarly engraved lid. The box was wrapped with a simple piece of rope twine that had been awkwardly tied in a bow. She noted that it was similar to the twine she had discovered in the root cellar. The deputy paused before she opened it to be sure Wink was near enough to see its contents. The two of them seemed to hold their breath as Toni slowly untied the parcel and lifted the wooden lid. A piece of tissue paper was folded neatly inside the box to hide and protect its treasure. As she gently lifted the edges of the paper both she and Wink were amazed to find a long, beautiful, and delicate hand-painted silk scarf inside.

"Look at this amazing piece of art would you?" The deputy stated in amazement. "This is unbelievable. I just can't imagine such an elegant thing as this scarf being found in this deplorable old place. Wink, this man was so odd, don't you think? And he kept so many secrets locked up in this awful place." Wink Martin nodded his head in agreement as the deputy continued with her rambling statement. "He was brilliant and talented and created such tender and emotional sketches of these women, and yet he remained here alone for more than forty years. Talk about an extreme dichotomy – first the skull I found in the cellar and now this beautiful scarf. They just don't mix. None of it makes sense. It just seems to me that he lived such a sad and lonely life and yet at the same time he might have actually killed someone. It's hard to grasp such divergent facts. I guess that's what intrigues me about the study of the human psyche. There are no two people alike. It's the same for criminals and their victims. Each and every one is totally unlike the one before. Who was this man and why did he live here in this deplorable place, and who was the person in the cellar?"

Wink confessed with animation. "This whole deal has been driving me nuts for weeks, Toni, ever since I found him dead. I can't imagine what would cause a man to cut himself off from his own life like this and live in such terrible conditions; this place really sucks."

Wink's voice became more subdued as he began to share his inner most thoughts with Toni. "In fact I've been more than a little bit curious about him since I found him here alone in this mess. The truth is, sometimes it keeps me up at night knowing that I had the opportunity to learn his story during the five years that I delivered groceries to him, and I didn't even try. I regret that now. I feel terrible because I never even talked to the old man in all those years but I never hesitated to accept his twenty dollar tips."

"Try not to beat your-self up over it, Wink," Toni Canon said as she stood to give her young friend a much needed hug and a quick pat on the back. "And try not to take this so personally. There's only so much each of us can do in our lives and no one can change the past, not even God. What's done is done. It's the present you need to focus on."

As she pulled away from Wink, their eyes met, and the two of them stared at one another for a long exaggerated moment sharing an unspoken emotional connection. It was as if they were actually seeing one another for the first time as a man and a woman. In those few quiet moments Toni realized she and Wink had shared a brief glimpse into each other's soul. It was awkward and yet mesmerizing. A sudden flash of desire washed over Toni Canon and she felt her cheeks quickly flush with color. Hoping that Wink had not noticed, Toni straightened and stepped away from her companion with increasing embarrassment.

Hearing her own words of wisdom and yet feeling the sudden swirl of emotion toward Wink, Toni's thoughts were easily drawn back to her brother, Andrew. She felt the gold heart-shaped locket move slightly on its chain beneath her uniform blouse. For a brief second she swallowed hard against a lump that developed in her throat as she traced her fingers gently over the outline of the locket. Toni had worn the locket every day since Andrew's death. It was her private badge of courage. She had learned about grief and heartache at a young age and she sensed that Wink Martin had done the same.

Even so, she definitely did not want her sudden burst of passion to get in the way of their working relationship. She was a professional and reminded herself quietly of that fact. "Let's call it a day and get out of here," she said quickly. "It's time for a break and I need to get this evidence to the sheriff. Hopefully this new information will be something really significant, and maybe there will be some news from forensics about the identity of the skull."

As Toni and Wink left the old codger's residence, a strong gust of wind suddenly swirled in the barren dirt in front of them. The fast-paced whirlwind blew dust particles into their faces and eyes as they huddled together to protect themselves from the blowing Nevada sand. Wink stood very near Toni with his arms wrapped around her in an effort to shield her from the blowing debris. It was a natural motion for a gentleman, especially since the deputy had her arms full of evidence boxes, but their awkward closeness intensified the sudden physical attraction Toni was feeling. Once again she felt a burning desire sweep through her body as Wink held his lean and fit frame against her, encompassing her entire being. She felt incredibly feminine and completely protected by his physical presence towering over her.

It was an odd sensation for Toni and one that she had not experienced before in her independent adult life. During the years since Andrew's death she had not allowed herself to become emotionally entangled with anyone while she built her law enforcement career. Toni had truly loved only one man in her life and he was gone from her forever. She did not intend to risk those feelings with an emotional connection to anyone else ever again. Besides, she did not consider herself to be a romantic woman and had no intention of becoming vulnerable and infatuated with any man. After all, she was the one carrying the gun and defending justice.

In spite of her resolute denial of physical attraction, she noted that Wink was really quite tall and very handsome and the scent of his cologne was truly wonderful. Toni suddenly recognized the familiar and tantalizing scent. It was *Aramis,* the same fragrance that her beloved brother Andrew had always worn. Oh God, how she had loved the smell of Andrew…..

With her eyes squeezed tightly closed, she quietly inhaled the enticing aroma of Wink Martin's cologne. Her heart pounded in her chest as memories of Andrew collided with her present reality. The deputy was nearly dizzy with emotion. Warm old memories and hot new sexual desires swirled inside her mind although her knees were weak and trembling. She quickly imagined herself falling into Wink's arms with rapture. Now you're being totally ridiculous she cautioned herself as Wink released his grip on her shoulders. Secretly Toni wondered if Wink might be feeling the same overwhelming attraction.

"Are you ok Toni?"

"Yes, I guess so. I just got dusted up a little," she laughed in a lame attempt to cover-up her spicy thoughts of him. "Thanks for your assistance. How about you, are you ok?"

Wink just nodded in the affirmative.

As the whirlwind dissipated against the old adobe cabin, several of the professor's handmade wind chimes clanged in concert with one another almost like ringing church bells. It

Dangerous Intentions

was quite eerie and seemed as if the ghostly spirits were suddenly announcing their arrival.

One of Chappy Morgan's birdhouses suddenly crashed violently to the ground from its perch nearby and collapsed into pieces only a few feet from where Toni and Wink were standing. Luckily the loud distraction immediately changed the focus of the deputy's attention. Toni was startled, to say the least, as she jumped with fear and maybe from too much raw sexual tension. She was dumfounded by what she saw. Wink, on the other hand, was fascinated by the impromptu racket the wind chimes made as he stared at the keys and chain links hanging over the cabin's front door.

"Honest to Pete that scared me!" she mused as she caught her breath. Do you see what I see right over there? Oh my God, I'm not imagining things, am I, Wink?"

"No, ma'am you certainly are not! It sure looks like we've uncovered another dark secret, Deputy. And that whole deal with the clattering wind chimes happening at the same moment the bird house crashed to the ground was a bit spooky if you ask me. It was like some big restless spirit just swirled in and made its presence known. Strange how things work out isn't it - and ever so true that providence works in super mysterious ways! Wow, listen to me, I sound like a religious spook! Seriously though, Toni, I am trembling inside clear to my toes."

Within a few feet of where the two were standing lay the exact black and orange license plate Toni and Wink had discovered in Chappy's drawings. It had long served as the roof on one of the professor's birdhouses. It was California 5GKQ436.

Chapter 35

The sheriff department's national computer data base provided a possible two-hundred choices of the 222 Sea Mist Drive address for the deputy to investigate. They were located across the entire nation with twenty-seven of the addresses listed in California alone.

The West coast offered the closest beach front property where Toni Canon chose to focus the address search. Additionally, the souvenir cable car from the San Francisco Wharf played an important role in her decision to focus on the bay area.

"This is progress, Sheriff," the deputy reported with enthusiasm. "By process of elimination and with some boots on the ground we may discover something about this man's family by the end of the week. I've got our computer techs doing some intensive work on these addresses in California first. They are finding property owner's names and telephone numbers."

"That's good work, Toni," the sheriff responded pleased with his young deputy's attitude. "We need to keep plugging along at this one so we can get this money and immense collection of books and drawings to their proper owner." Yes, Sir," the deputy agreed, "It's become an interesting search.

Wink Martin has been a lot of help, and we're doing our best to get this mystery ironed out as soon as possible. I just hope that we get a break soon on the identity of the skull I found in Morgan's cellar."

"Toni, all we know at this point is that it is believed to be that of an Asian male, approximately thirty-five to forty-five years of age and it was estimated to have been in that cellar thirty to forty years or more. All missing person reports from that long ago are definitely cold cases now. Science is making amazing progress these days with DNA testing and forensic reconstruction. We'll know more soon, I'm certain of it. I'm going to authorize a full search of the Morgan property. We need to get inside that old outhouse pit and do a thorough ground search of the land inside his fence. My gut tells me there's a lot more to this story that we haven't uncovered yet. Morgan was an intriguing old man with a lot of secrets. It's time we learned about some of them."

Days later Deputy Canon was not deterred in her search of the old man's property. She personally searched page by page through numerous notebooks until she came upon a notebook of drawings entitled *American White Pelicans* where she discovered another of Chappy's personal pencil drawings. In the sketch, an elderly woman wore a kind face and gentle eyes that were softly framed by wisps of hair that had fallen loose from a bun worn high on her head. She wore a large round locket around her neck which was engraved with the initials *IJ* and there was a sailing ship's mast in the background as seen through a large picture window.

"One more piece of the puzzle, Mr. Morgan, you secretive old rascal!" the deputy declared. "I'm going to figure this out one way or another. You can bet on that!"

At the end of another long day of searching page by page, Deputy Canon was ready to call it quits when she found one more odd drawing in an unnamed notebook.

She guessed it to be the sketch of an older model El Camino Chevrolet with what appeared to be the word "bochar" or "hochar" or something similar printed on the license plate. And *End of the road* was scribbled across the paper which Toni found unusual. The professor's printing in every other notebook was perfectly mechanical. It seemed strange to see such sloppiness.

The words had obviously been erased and rewritten several times and were ultimately left on the page but they were badly smudged. The words "El Camino" were clearly marked on the truck's tail gate in the sketch as if the vehicle was being driven away from the viewer. Toni was intrigued as the sketch offered one more clue to the mystery of the illusive Charles Morgan.

The search of the California address was frustrating and time consuming and provided very few leads. Most of the properties had been built or purchased within the last twenty years and none of the owners contacted had any knowledge of the illusive Charles Morgan. Months after the death of the old recluse the investigation appeared cold.

On a hot weekend in late September, Toni Canon decided to give the California addresses another try. Some of the telephone numbers were unlisted and the necessary paperwork for legal authorization had prolonged the department's access to them. Because of the cable car souvenir found in Chappy's root cellar, Toni felt certain the San Francisco area was the place to begin calling the unlisted numbers.

The first number dialed was disconnected. The second number belonged to a Kim Chong who had no knowledge of Mr. Morgan and who had purchased the property only a month earlier. Frustrated, she dialed the third number, associated with a property in Monterey, California in the name of C. A. Righetti.

"Hello, Righetti residence, may I help you?" A woman's voice answered with a heavy Italian accent. Toni was surprised by the voice and stuttered briefly as she collected her thoughts and asked if she was the owner of the house. "No, no. Ms. Righetti not home. Is message?" the gruff voice asked.

"Yes ma'am, could you please ask Ms. Righetti to contact Toni Canon at the sheriff's department in Nevada as soon as possible at 555-234-1299. It is very important that I speak with her. Do you understand me and did you get the number?"

"Si, Si, cinque cinque cinque, due tre quattro, uno due nove nove. Sorry," the woman added in English.

"555-234-1299. Si, Si, Toni Canon, la polizia. Grazie Grazie. Thank you. Arrivederci."

"Thank you very much ma'am," Toni responded officially, "I hope to hear from Ms. Righetti soon."

Chapter 36

Caroline Righetti never married. A striking silver-haired beauty at the age of seventy-eight, she spent most of her time in recent years carefully tending the variety of flowers that bloom in her garden beside the sea. Hers was a quiet life, one that she chose for herself in 1963. In the beginning, there were the occasional trips to the theater district in San Francisco with Simon Pearle and the countless tedious meetings at various museums regarding fundraising. But for the most part, Caroline became a recluse in her own refuge at 222 Sea Mist Drive.

In the early days after Chappy left her so unexpectedly, Caroline made persistent inquiries of Simon Pearle as to the blond man's whereabouts. She begged and pleaded with the French attorney for any tiny bit of information that he could share with her but there was none. Simon swore on all things holy that he didn't know where Chappy had gone. He had simply disappeared off the face of the earth.

Caroline had no choice but to believe Simon when the news that she was carrying the professor's child made no difference in the attorney's final answer about Doctor Morgan's absence. Caroline was devastated by the lack of information. Simon was also distraught about his friend's disappearance and hired three different private detectives to search for the missing man during the first years of Morgan's disappearance. But he slowly became convinced that the first investigator, a squirrely little character named Moe Stackman, simply absconded with the fees that Simon had paid him in advance. The attorney never heard another word from the wannabe private eye.

The second man that Simon hired was a colorful figure from Chinatown. As a member of a major Chinese crime family, Ho Chan Wang was unreliable at best. But Simon had regarded his connections with the underbelly of the city to be invaluable in a search for someone who didn't want to be found. The Aisan man was a professional thug but he also disappeared with a great deal of Simon Pearle's money. It was not known if Wang was actually dead or was in hiding after a violent gang dispute erupted in Chinatown. The Chinese community remained very tight-lipped and secretive which only complicated Simon Pearle's efforts. He knew the Chinese people were afraid of retaliation against their families and businesses if any information about Ho Chan Wang was divulged. It had been a costly mistake to involve the gangster in the first place.

The third and final investigator that was hired had at least provided Simon with a bit of hopeful information regarding Professor Charles Morgan. Sam Thomas told Mr. Pearle about a gentleman in Sacramento, California who recognized Charles Morgan's photograph and who had talked briefly with the professor about his 1963 gold Avanti automobile. They had struck up a casual conversation at a gas station where Charles Morgan had given the man one-hundred dollars for gas and food. The man was naturally impressed by the Good Samaritan and remembered the professor distinctly because of his generosity and the beautiful car he was driving. The Avanti headed east on US Hwy. 40 and that's all the man could relate to the investigator.

After that information was given to Simon Pearle, the search for Chappy Morgan had gone cold.

Sam Thomas retired and moved to a small town in Montana which left Simon frustrated and unhappy. It was quite obvious that Chappy simply did not want to be found and there seemed to be no trace of him.

Caroline, safely guarded in her exclusive and secluded residence near the sea, managed to keep herself from the long reach of her father's arm. The belligerent man continued with his distasteful lifestyle however, and his photographs often appeared in the Daily Chronicle which privately embarrassed and humiliated her.

One day, in the early winter of 1963, the repulsive Fredrick Winston climbed out of his chauffeured limousine in front of his usual Nob Hill hotel with a painted young harlot on his arm. Of course he somehow managed to be surrounded by a horde of local photographers at just the precise moment of his arrival. Naturally the pictures of her father and the young prostitute promptly appeared in the society pages much to Caroline's chagrin.

What she couldn't see in the photographs, however, happened in the few moments after the cameras and flash bulbs were all gone. The rotund Winston and his redheaded whore were approached by a disheveled street beggar just as the California sun was setting. In his usual loud and vulgar style, Winston belittled the poorly dressed blond man as he ordered him off the premises and out of his sight. In the process of adding insult to injury, Winston rudely tossed the indigent a silver dollar which bounced musically on the concrete sidewalk before rolling to a slow stop at the dirty man's feet.

With a sly smile the beggar quickly picked up the coin and tossed the large silver piece high into the air with a flick of his thumb. Laughing hysterically, he then dramatically retrieved the coin in mid-air and quickly slapped it down on the back of his left hand as if playing a game of heads-or-tails. With the impressive flare of a pantomime artist, the beggar silently slid the single silver dollar into his ragged trouser pocket as Fredrick

Winston stood by silently quite mesmerized by the stranger's odd behavior.

As Winston finally stepped toward the hotel's revolving door with the redheaded woman close on his heels, the disheveled beggar suddenly offered up a full bottle of cognac to the couple. He had retrieved the shiny bottle from a deep pocket inside his long shabby overcoat. With the same arrogance and brashness seen in his personal and financial dealings, Winston grabbed the bottle from the filthy vagabond, lifted it to his lips, and proceeded to chug more than half its contents with a single breath. Afterward, he exhaled a loud disgusting belch and patted his huge round belly in delight.

The redheaded harlot then took her turn with the cool dark liquid and laughingly tossed the nearly empty bottle back to the disheveled stranger standing on the sidewalk. The bottle, laced with a heavy concentration of cocaine and barbiturates fell short of the beggar's outstretched hands. It crashed onto the pavement leaving glass and cognac splattered in a spider web design near the back tires of Winston's limousine.

Within seconds, the beggar abruptly turned on his heels and disappeared from sight with a loud wicked laugh trailing behind him. The fat man and his whore watched in disbelief from the busy street on Nob Hill. The shattered bottle was simply left for the morning street sweeper.

Fredrick Winston died of heart failure later that same night as a result of a narcotic overdose. Questions remained whether it was an accidental death or a possible homicide. Adding to the mystery, Winston's female companion disappeared from the city after her own recovery and release from the hospital. Even though she had been in critical condition, she would not or more likely could not provide the police with an accurate statement regarding their nefarious activities on Nob Hill. The vulgar Winston had been consorting with the redheaded prostitute in his elegant suite atop the famous hotel when his nude, drunken, and severely glutinous body was found in a king-sized four-poster bed adorned with imported satins and brocade. Law enforcement officials were baffled by the fact that there were no traces of heroin or cocaine found in the magnificent suite when the police arrived at the scene. And no drug paraphernalia of any sort was ever found in the couple's personal belongings.

It could only be surmised that Winston and his whore had consumed the vast quantity of tainted drugs prior to their arrival at the hotel. The short obese man had rejoiced in his presumed victory over Charles Morgan with many different women, all of whom were prostitutes. He always held his clandestine meetings atop luxury hotels. But the stylish locations with elegant furnishings and beautiful views of the City by the Bay did little to alter the seamy side of life the vulgar and disgusting multi-millionaire enjoyed. He was more than pleased the self-righteous professor was gone and virtually forgotten. And he nearly drank himself to death in celebration of that fact long before his heart actually gave out on Nob Hill.

Caroline was heavy with child at the time of the obscene old man's death and she chose not to hold a ceremonial funeral service for her father. Instead she cremated his body and privately inurned his ashes in the family mausoleum in San Francisco. She had not seen the repulsive man in person since the terrible incident with Chappy and Simon Pearle after the silk scarf celebration. As far as she could discern her father didn't know that she was pregnant with the professor's child.

The old man's death was bittersweet for Caroline. The man she loved left San Francisco to protect her from the foul-mouthed and belligerent Fredrick Winston and his large array of goons. Since her father was dead there was no further need for Chappy to be gone. Her suffering in his absence seemed meaningless and unnecessary. Caroline was heart-broken and clueless about where to look for the only man she ever loved. Her father was dead but Chappy was gone and none of it made any sense to the exquisite Caroline Righetti.

Chapter 37

Ivy Marie Righetti was born in the winter of 1963. She was a beautiful baby with chubby little cheeks, curly auburn hair, and cobalt blue eyes. Simon, Lionel, and Laurel were all there to support Caroline when the baby girl was born. They were Caroline's family through thick and thin and she loved them dearly. The three of them, along with her tiny new baby, were the only links to the illusive Charles Morgan that Caroline Righetti could cling to.

Doctor Righetti did not practice medicine again after Ivy's birth although she always intended to return one day. Life with her happy and energetic daughter consumed her thoughts and filled her days with so much love there was no longer room in her life for cardiology.

Mother and daughter spent long hours enjoying the beach, collecting sea shells, and watching the sea with its soothing and never-ending waves. It was a constant joy for Caroline to watch the effervescent auburn-haired Ivy as she skipped through her childhood with boundless energy and affection. There was no limit to the child's sense of wonder and delight at the world around her and no way that Caroline was going to miss a single moment of her daughter's life.

Caroline found peace in the solitude of the seaside retreat Chappy had given her. As the days grew into months and years, Caroline became wholly entrenched as Ivy's single parent attending school functions, music recitals, and theater rehearsals. She arranged for play dates and sleepovers and Ivy's horse riding lessons. Her life was busy and fulfilling even though she sacrificed her love of medicine in the process.

Not a single day went by for Caroline, however, without thoughts of Chappy Morgan invading her mind. He was constantly with her and she longed for him to share their beautiful child as Ivy blossomed into a lovely young woman. She chose Ivy's name because of the stories Chappy had shared with her about his loving Grandmother Ivy Johannson. Although it broke her heart that Chappy abandoned them both, she felt a strong spiritual and emotional bond to the missing man simply because of Ivy's name.

Caroline and Chappy Morgan were kindred spirits and eternal soul mates. Nothing changed that.

Chapter 38

Ivy Marie Righetti on the other hand, became a very spirited and high-strung redhead with a sense of restlessness that she could not explain. She was moody and animated with a dramatic flair that swung from miserably deep depressions to unrealistically lofty heights.

She attended several colleges and studied various subjects, but none satisfied her sense of longing and discontent. She shared many lovers, both men and women, and tossed them out one by one as she had with her unwanted trash. Caroline suspected that Ivy was experimenting with illegal drugs and detected the signs of addiction on several occasions. But Ivy would not listen to a word her mother said about seeing a counselor or physician for help.

Ivy was indignant about the secrets her mother kept and on occasion she became belligerent and obsessive about the issue. She would cut herself off from her mother in protest with hostile words and cruel accusations and then just as suddenly she would reappear repentant as if nothing was wrong between the two of them.

Caroline was at a loss about how to deal with her temperamental and extremely volatile daughter.

Ivy was thrilled, however, with the opportunity to travel to Europe with her mother for her twentieth birthday as Caroline struggled to maintain a close relationship with her enchanting and unruly daughter. At times their relationship was stressed to the limit and beyond as Ivy seemed to be cut from very different and unusual cloth. But Caroline always tried her best to keep the lines of communication open between the two of them.

Caroline kept her daughter from the truth about who her father was and how he abandoned them. She thought it was best to protect her from the sad and disquieting fact that she and Chappy never married. Ivy was resentful and antagonistic toward her mother and Caroline finally realized that perhaps she misjudged her daughter by trying to shelter her from the truth.

Gradually she told Ivy the details of her life without naming Chappy during their trip to visit their Righetti relatives in Italy. Ivy fell in love with the story of the hand-painted silk scarf and the music of 'Peggy Sue'. Eventually she began to see her mother through different eyes with more respect and tender affection. She better understood their isolated life in Monterey and gained an appreciation for her mother's dedication and strength. Ivy also began, however, to feel a sad regret that her mother, the exquisite Caroline, had not lived her own life fully with the love and happiness of the man she loved and the father Ivy so badly craved for herself. But the unselfish and understanding side of Ivy was short lived and her true colors soon emerged once again with hostile rage and discontent. Ivy spiraled out of control as her drug use continued.

Caroline returned to her beloved seaside home the following spring without the redheaded Ivy. Her daughter had fallen in love with Italy and its handsome men as well as the romantic life she imagined for herself as a painter. Ivy discovered she was a naturally gifted and talented artist and the Italian countryside seemed the idyllic place for the free spirited young woman to master her craft and find her own way in the world. After all, Caroline had done all she could for the unappreciative, fickle, and frivolous Ivy Righetti.

Fredrick Winston's colossal wealth made it possible for Ivy to do as she pleased with the enormous trust fund Caroline set up for her when she turned twenty-one. There was no doubt Ivy would be reckless and silly with her new found fortune as she had no sense of family value or personal integrity.

She was an easy target amongst the reprehensible European men who eagerly took advantage of her youth and social ineptitude. So it was with a sense of sadness and loss that Caroline found herself alone again in her seaside seclusion.

Little by little, she began to immerse herself in the world of fine arts as a productive and yet indirect way of staying connected to her beautiful and illusive daughter.

Chapter 39

In 1985, more than twenty years after Chappy Morgan left his home on the hill, Lionel Carver lay near death in the magnificent old house overlooking the San Francisco Bay. It was the last time Caroline would visit with him.

Lionel and his wife Laurel had become two of her dearest friends but the beautiful doctor had not stepped foot inside the stately old mansion since the spring of 1963. Her heart was heavy with mixed emotions as she entered the home she once shared with Chappy Morgan and she was immediately confronted with a flood of memories.

Caroline paused for a moment to survey the changes the Carvers had made inside of the old house and she was pleasantly surprised to note there were not many. Only a few pieces of furniture replaced the fine antiques she had taken with her to her new home in Monterey. The wall paper and fine carpet remained exactly the same and most of the artwork seemed familiar.

Caroline's eyes misted a little as she remembered all that she had experienced in the grand old home. She and Chappy were very happy there for a time and so much in love. Her daughter Ivy was conceived there and her medical career had flourished while she lived with Chappy. As the memories washed over her,

Caroline recalled her last moments with Charles Morgan and a sense of loneliness once again filled her being.

Suddenly the day's reality intervened as Laurel interrupted Caroline's train of thought when she reached out to greet her.

"Hello, Dear, thank-you for coming. Lionel has been waiting to speak with you for several days now. I think he has actually been holding on to life until he could see you again."

Laurel's words affected Caroline significantly as she struggled to keep her composure. She was already too emotional with her visit to the house and Laurel's sympathetic greeting pushed her beyond the point of tears.

"Thank-you, Laurel, that's very kind of you to say. How are you doing?"

"I'm fine dear, just fine. We have Lionel in the large bedroom. I'll leave the two of you to talk. Stay as long as you like, Caroline. I'm afraid he hasn't much strength left but he insisted on speaking with you one more time."

Caroline inhaled deeply as she entered the bedroom she had shared with Chappy Morgan so long ago. It was all she could do to maintain her composure as the walls of the poorly lit room seemed to close in on her.

Lionel was propped up on several soft pillows and she could see there was still a twinkle in his eyes as he smiled and signaled her close to the bed. After a brief hug, the elderly man asked for a drink of water and then patted the bed where he wanted Caroline to sit.

Lionel could not speak above a whisper. "You look as beautiful as ever Caroline and I am so glad you came to see me."

Caroline said nothing as she swallowed hard against the lump in her throat. She just smiled. She didn't dare try to speak. This visit was much more difficult than she realized. She was not prepared for the emotional response her old home inspired and it was terribly sad for her to see her longtime friend in such poor condition. None of her medical training had equipped her for such an emotional scene.

"I want to apologize to you Caroline for my family's weakness. Mr. Charles was always so good to me and I promised him I would look after you. I know I've let both of you down. I never wanted any of our personal ugliness to touch your life. I know how much you love Ivy Marie and it breaks my heart to know that no-good son of mine hurt your precious baby girl. I am so ashamed that Wilson brought his drug business back from Viet Nam. If he was here right now I'd beat the living tar out of him! I just thank the Lord every day his mama did not live to see what he became. He ruined his own boy Leroy and so many others. And that damn boy got Ivy tangled up in all the dirty business of using drugs. She was always weak but she's a good girl. Please forgive me, Caroline, I wish I could change everything."

"It's okay Lionel, there's nothing for you to apologize for. I thank you for your concern, but there is nothing any of us can do about Ivy. She has a wild spirit that can't be tamed and she makes all of her own choices. It was a terrible mistake for me to give her free access to so much money when she was so young.......but that cannot be changed now. We just do the best we can. Please don't worry yourself about anything. We are who we are Lionel, that's just the way it is. I love you and I want you to rest easy."

Caroline left the beautiful old house on the hill overlooking the San Francisco Bay knowing that she would not be seeing Lionel again nor would she visit her old neighborhood a second time. The dying man's words were a haunting reminder to Caroline that her daughter Ivy was in serious trouble. The sad reality was Ivy refused her mother's help time and again and Caroline felt powerless to do anything about it. Ivy was systematically destroying everything good in her life.

Over the years, Caroline had heard plenty of rumors. They were ugly rumors about tall skinny Wilson Carver, known as

Jangles to his friends. He was a major drug dealer in the black community long before he suddenly turned up missing twenty years earlier. He had earned the reputation of being violent with his underlings and vicious with his competitors. He was successful and wealthy and terribly addicted to his own product for most of his life. But worse than all his criminal involvements, Caroline knew he had been terribly unkind to his own father, Lionel.

Wilson carried a large collection of keys on several links of chain that chimed together whenever he walked. Caroline assumed his nickname Jangles probably came from that trivial activity which had begun during his days in Viet Nam.

She also knew the pock-faced Jangles once had some sort of business arrangement with her father, the late Fredrick Winston, although she was never certain of the exact nature of their relationship. In spite of his prominent position in society, Winston was known to have dealt with some real creepy and unethical criminal types. Lionel Carver, in the meantime, was the salt-of-the-earth and one of her dearest friends. Caroline simply could not believe that Lionel's son Wilson "Jangles" Carver could actually have shared a single drop of Lionel's blood.

And then, of course, there was Lionel's grandson - Wilson Carver's son - the ever disgusting Leroy Jangles Carver. The mere thought of him made Caroline's skin crawl. He had followed in his father's footsteps in the illegal drug trade when he was only a teenager. She surmised that he was the despicable character still selling drugs to her lovely Ivy Marie. Caroline remembered him as an obnoxious and revolting being after her single meeting with him. He was a callous and overweight man who became an incredibly slick businessman.

The elegant Caroline had been alarmed by his rudeness and violent demeanor. She became afraid of him instantly. There was little doubt that her daughter's relationship with Lionel's grandson was very unhealthy and very illegal.

On her drive back to Monterey, Caroline became quite melancholy. She was losing two of her most trusted allies at nearly the same time. Simon Pearle, her most revered comrade and loyal friend had unexpectedly suffered a massive coronary a few days earlier and his death was imminent. With Lionel Carver on his deathbed, Caroline sensed that life would never be the same.

Her old friends were leaving her one by one and along with them they were taking so many precious memories of her beloved Chappy Morgan.

Chapter 40

Wink Martin arrived at the sheriff's office quite late as Deputy Canon was making phone calls to narrow the search of the 222 Sea Mist Drive address list. As he plopped down in the chair next to her, he absent mindedly picked up the telephone list she was working from. As he quickly scanned the names and telephone numbers typed on the white sheet of paper, the name Righetti suddenly and unexpectedly caught his attention. He felt hot with emotion. The young man leaned back in his chair and clasped his hands on top of his head as his heart pounded in his chest. He twirled himself around and around in the office chair until he finally caught Toni's attention as she hung up the telephone.

"What's up Wink? You're white as a ghost," the deputy inquired.

"I can't believe this list of names." Wink responded feeling sick to his stomach.

"Oh, man I've had an eerie feeling about this deal ever since we found that sketch of the woman inscribed with 222 Sea Mist Drive. I'm almost scared to tell you Toni, but I think I know who that woman is."

"Well don't stop now," Toni urged, "Come on Wink, give it up. Who is she?"

Taking a deep breath, Wink began to relay the facts of his life as best he could to Toni Canon.

"My Grandmother's name is Caroline Righetti and she lives in Monterey, California. Just like on the list here, C.A. Righetti. I don't remember her address but her name is definitely Righetti. My Mom is Ivy Righetti-D'Angelo."

"Oh God, I feel sick to my stomach. I think I'm going to puke."

"Here drink some water, Toni said as she quickly collected a bottle of water from the office fridge. Get your head below your knees for a minute, take a couple of deep breaths, and let's sort this out. Tell me what you know. This could be the answer we're looking for, Wink, you could be the only one to solve this puzzle."

Wink hesitated and said, "I don't know, Toni, this leads to so much shit in my own life that I've worked hard to forget over the years. I'm afraid to open the can of worms I know this will lead to for fear it will ruin everything I've got going for me now. I knew it would all come back to haunt me one day. Fuck! I can't believe this. Sorry about the language, but I had a real bad feeling about this the other day and it's been nagging at me ever since. I guess there's no way out of it now is there? I just need to suck it up and spit it all out there one word at a time. I'm not sure I can get through it, Toni. This really does suck!"

"Maybe you don't know this Wink, but there's a Bible verse that states: *Then you will know the truth, and the truth will set you free.* I'll help you, Wink, we'll sort this out together. All you have to do is trust me."

Chapter 41

Gabriele Martin D'Angelo had arrived in Sausalito, California from Naples, Italy with his mother when he was twelve years old. He was named after his maternal great great grandfather, Gabriele Robustelli and his Italian father, Martin D'Angelo. He was always a rebellious kid who had pretty much grown-up unattended on the streets of Naples and Rome while his mother entertained one man after another as she moved between cities and art studios.

Young Gabriele had no memory of his father although they lived together as a family in Portofino until he was two years old. He was a street-smart and savvy boy who always had plenty of money to spend. But he liked the camaraderie he found with the Italian boys on the dark narrow streets of Italy. He would sneak away from his private school at night to hang around with the older crowds of teenagers and eventually he joined one of their gangs: *I Ragazzi Della Notte, The Boys of the Night.*

Starved for attention and wise beyond his years, young Gabriele D'Angelo was an unsuspecting thief who achieved popularity with the teenagers by becoming an amazingly proficient pickpocket. He often gave the money he stole to the less fortunate kids in his circle of friends which endeared him to them on a grand scale. He was handsome and charming with the look of a complete innocent with his wide cobalt blue eyes and blond curly hair. But his nimble fingers and lightning quick feet proved him a talented and prosperous thief at a very young age.

His fellow thieves named him *Wink* because he could look the largest of women and the toughest of men straight in the eye. With a disarming wink he would steal their wallets, purses, or miscellaneous goods, blow them a kiss and be gone in the blink of an eye. He liked the American nickname, *Wink*, and took it as his own from that moment on.

Sausalito, California proved to be a very unhappy and unhealthy place for Wink as his mother opened yet another upscale art studio and had several more lovers not much older than he. They lived on a large and beautiful houseboat in the exclusive Paradise Marina where Wink was naturally drawn to a drug using group of well-to-do teenagers whose parents were mostly inattentive artists, attorneys, and doctors of one sort or another.

As the youngest candidate of yet another street gang, the elite *Streetsliders*, he was required to pass their initiation test before he could become a full-fledged member. Wink successfully accomplished that task by lifting the wallets from not one, as was required, but from three attorneys while they waited for court to open in the downtown municipal complex. He was hailed as a hero and was often asked to repeat his successful stunt whenever one of the gang's leaders needed something worth stealing. He was, after all, a consummate and experienced international thief by the age of thirteen. He was also a drug addicted and melancholy young man who hated his mother at least as much as his own pointless life.

Ivy Righetti unwisely burned through a large portion of her inheritance by the time she was thirty-five. Over the course of ten years she sponsored several promising Italian artists and musicians who managed to steal her affections.

They took advantage of her wealth, and left her heart-broken and disillusioned. Eventually, this sad course of action led her back to California where she repeated the same process all over again but with American men instead.

Ivy was out of touch with reality in those days as she too spent much of her life in a drug induced stupor. She claimed that drugs inspired her artistic creativity and her romantic nature. But the truth of the matter was they kept her mind and emotions numbed and unresponsive to the needs of her young teenaged son not to mention the needs of her own mother. Although her art studio was very successful, her personal life was a disaster.

Even the elegant Caroline was unable to intervene on her daughter's and grandson's behalf because of the body guards and lovers constantly surrounding Ivy. It was a sad state of affairs that continued for five more long and depressing years.

A few days before Wink's seventeenth birthday, Ivy arranged an exclusive art show featuring several artists' work in addition to her own paintings of the Italian countryside. The coliseum was filled with very expensive jewelry, hand-blown pottery, bronze sculptures, and hand-painted china along with Ivy's wonderful collection of oil paintings. The grand affair was attended by a large crowd of interested and wealthy buyers from around the world.

As Wink wandered through the gathering of artists and rich art connoisseurs, he suddenly recognized a well-dressed and intimidating black man arguing with his mother as they entered her private office at the back of the building. He had seen the same man from a distance when *The Streetsliders* had done some illegal business with him a few weeks earlier. As skillfully as he had done during some of his preeminent heists, Wink gained access to the office area where he could over-hear the heated conversation without being seen.

To his dismay, the disagreement was over cocaine. The disagreement involved the shipment his mother was expecting and the amount of money she was willing to pay. The burly black man was adamant the deal had changed and the price had gone up.

"Fuck this, Ivy. Take it or leave it! I don't give a damn. You know this shit is primo and I've got plenty of buyers."

The man spoke callously as he slammed the briefcase down on the desk. Wink's mother begged the big man with nauseating baby talk but the insulting man just stood there with his arms crossed in defiance. After several minutes of negotiating, Ivy finally relented as she retrieved a bag of money from her office safe and slammed it down on the desk. In turn, she wanted the drug dealer to go with her to get the additional money needed which she kept at her house-boat a few miles across town.

With an arrogant smile the man foolishly agreed as Ivy seductively danced in front of him like a cheap hooker. She shrewdly danced around him as she cleverly mimicked the 1968 Jerry Jeff Walker song of *Mr. Bojangles*.

> "*I knew a man - Roy Jangles - and he'd dance for you.....*
> *O Mister Roy Jangles - let's dance, dance, dance.*"

The fat man just laughed and called her a red-headed whore as Ivy twirled around dancing. She unbuttoned her silk blouse to reveal her large ample breasts and continued with her lap dance as she teased and fawned over him rubbing his bulging genitals and kissing his ear. After slowly removing his Armani suit jacket and tie, she ceremoniously unbuttoned his crisp white shirt and began to stroke his hairy chest as she licked his dark-skinned over-fed belly with an undulating tongue.

The big man was definitely turned on with her enticements as he impatiently fondled her breasts and brazenly grabbed at her crotch. Wink watched in disgust from his hidden location. He could hear the vulgar and disrespectful words the scar-faced man spoke to his mother but she just laughed it off and encouraged him shamelessly.

It was a sickening display and one Wink had seen far too often as he continued to spy on his mother through the atrium window. In the heat of lust, the ringing telephone interrupted Ivy's sexual escapade. Immediately after a brief telephone conversation the laughing duo shared several lines of cocaine and then conveniently and carelessly left Ivy's bag of cash and the black leather briefcase under the desk inside the locked office. Within minutes after the call, the giddy duo left the building groping one another and exchanging rude and obscene comments as they hastily wiped their noses, readjusted their clothes, and climbed into the waiting limo.

In the next moment Wink decided that the rewards in the office were his for the taking regardless of the consequences. He was thoroughly disgusted with his mother's antics, tired of the unending parade of men, and sick of his meaningless life in the Paradise Marina. He easily picked the door lock, snuck into the office, and gathered the stash of drugs and cash without a single eye upon him.

The Streetslider hadn't lost his touch....

Wink spent the next three days running and hiding in the cold damp San Francisco night with the homeless dregs of society. He shared the stolen cocaine with men, women, and runaway teenagers to insure his safety from the police and other drug dealers as well.

Most of the cash from his mother's ill-fated drug deal was ironically stolen from him during his three-day binging stupor along with his personal items of clothing. He lost his wallet and identification and spent seventy-two long hours in a state of semi-consciousness. He was hidden in the city's worst derelict neighborhood on a filthy mattress in a cardboard box while police and ambulance sirens screamed around him. But he survived.

On the morning of his seventeenth birthday he somehow managed to get himself aboard an empty railroad car where he was eventually dumped like trash alongside of the tracks in Fallon, Nevada.

Known only as Wink Martin after his ungracious arrival, his life was ultimately saved by Jesse and Elena Garcia in the little trailer behind the race track stables.

Chapter 42

Caroline Righetti returned Toni Canon's phone call the day after Wink Martin bared his soul. It was an astounding turn of events and one that was not wasted on the sheriff or his young deputy.

A trip to Monterey was the next logical step in the official investigation, and yet the entire story of Chappy Morgan and Wink Martin had become a personal issue for the sheriff and Toni Canon. They both felt an unspoken responsibility to protect the likable young man they had come to know and respect.

It was becoming clear that the link between the deceased old codger and Wink Martin might represent a family connection, not to mention, the young man's possible inheritance of an immense fortune.

During the telephone call with Ms. Righetti, Toni chose her words carefully as she inquired about Caroline's relationship with Charles Morgan.

Toward the end of their conversation she informed Ms. Righetti that Mr. Morgan was recently deceased. And that a pencil sketch had been found among his belongings with her address of 222 Sea Mist Drive inscribed on the drawing.

After she expressed her sympathy, Toni heard the heartache in Caroline's voice with the news of Morgan's death. And yet the older woman spoke with strong resolve and intelligent answers.

Yes, she had known Charles Preston Morgan personally. He was affectionately known to her as Chappy. He was a wonderful, intelligent, and gentle man who had been educated at Stanford University. They had lived together in San Francisco for several years until 1963 when he left without leaving a forwarding address.

She had given birth to his daughter, Ivy Marie Righetti that same year and they never heard from him again. Caroline informed Toni that Chappy also had a grandson, Gabriele Martin D'Angelo who had been killed quite tragically in some type of gang war over drugs several years earlier. Her daughter and grandson were the two people she wished Chappy could have known but sadly he had not. Hers was a gut-wrenching tale of broken hearts and lost love.

Chapter 43

Toni Canon arranged to meet Wink Martin for coffee at 6:00 p.m. the following evening. Her mind was a blur with questions. She knew her conversation with Wink would be a difficult one as she buoyed herself with her first cup of sweet blond coffee.

"Hi," she said easily as Wink joined her at the table. "Thanks for coming on such short notice."

"No problem, Deputy.....what's up?"

Toni inhaled deeply as she gently held onto the gold heart-shaped locket hanging around her neck. She suddenly needed her brother, Andrew's strength to guide her through the correct words for her friend Wink.

Gabriele Martin D'Angelo was a stranger to her and yet in her heart she knew him so well. Their relationship had become incredibly complicated overnight and Toni privately wished it had not happened. It was just a name after all, but she hadn't yet become comfortable with the facts of his identity. Gabriele D'Angelo and the story of his life and family was bizarre, to say the least, and Toni knew that the implications of his birthright would likely change everything for the two of them.

"I have some new information I want to share with you and I thought it might be easier to tell you in person."

"There's no easy way for me to say this, so I am just going to lay it out for you the best I can. I spoke with your Grandmother Caroline Righetti today and she confirmed what you suspected, that the 222 Sea Mist Drive address in Monterey is indeed hers. She also informed me that you were declared dead five years ago as the victim of a gang related drug war. That's why there is no missing person's report on you or anyone searching for you. She sadly believes you were killed that night. And, Wink, she did, in fact, know Charles Preston Morgan very well. I know this will probably require some serious thought, but Caroline told me that old man Morgan was Ivy's father and your grandfather."

Gabriele D'Angelo didn't move a muscle. He remained silent for several moments. He looked at Toni with cobalt blue eyes that searched the depths of her soul. She could see for herself that he was trying to process the information she had so bluntly reported and she suddenly wished she had chosen different words – kinder words.

Her first instinct was to reach out and comfort Wink, but her law enforcement training demanded restraint. She felt the overwhelming need to do or say something profound that would ease his pain and confusion, if only she knew exactly what that something was.

"I don't think your mother knows much about Chappy. Sorry, I mean Charles Morgan. At least that's the impression your grandmother left me with. It seems he left Caroline before your mom was born and they had no further contact with one another. I think it's quite a lovely and sad love story in its own way and one that seems to be unfinished now that you are a part of it. Please say something, Wink, I don't know what else I'm supposed to do here. I thought this would be easier for you if it came from me. Was I wrong?"

Wink Martin finally responded.

"I should have felt some sort of connection to him or something don't you think? Or at the very least I should have

Dangerous Intentions

been aware that there was some link between us. I must be stupid.....I mean really Toni, what are the chances that two random strangers can become a part of one another's life in a strange town far away from their former lives and not have a single clue about one other? That seems incredibly far-fetched. I was dumped off the train here. I didn't have the foggiest notion where I was at the time. Why was Morgan here when my grandmother was in the city? I saw him every month for the better part of five years and I never even had a conversation with the man! God, what kind of an ignorant ass can I be?"

After a long pause he continued. "You know, Toni, I intended to tell you this sometime ago, but I got a real bad vibe out at his place the day he died. His rocking chair has a belt on it with the name *Jangles* carved on it. I knew a man called Jangles in San Francisco. He was the drug dealer that supplied my mom and he was there that night when I stole her money and cocaine from her art gallery. Oh my God, Toni, how did that belt end up here? Did Morgan know Jangles? What's been going on with that old man for all these years? Was Morgan hiding from his life too – this boggles my mind."

"I don't even remember hearing his name when I was a kid. I can't believe this. My grandmother said nothing about him during the few occasions I saw her and neither did my mom. And it looks like he may have killed someone at that junk pile of his. What kind of people are we? He was an educated millionaire who lived alone here for forty-four years. And my grandmother that he left in San Francisco was alone there for the same length of time. And then there's the disgusting story of me and my mom running like gypsies, leaving my dad behind in Italy. Oh my God, we could have been a real family, an honest-to-God real family." His words trailed off to a mere whisper.

Wink responded to Toni's news with much more intensity than she thought he would. He was distraught, angry, and consumed with guilt. Tears welled in his eyes as he struggled to maintain his composure. He was teetering on the edge of a full-blown emotional breakdown and they both knew it. There seemed to be so much about his own life that he was not aware of and he suddenly wondered if his own drug use was the reason why.

"What a fucking mess," he stated flatly as he cradled his head in his hands.… "A stupid fucking mess."

Toni was still trying to be cool, calm, and collected but her stomach was tied in knots and her legs felt like jelly. "Please try not to blame yourself so much. How could you have known? Your childhood was a real disaster and you were very young. I know it's hard to believe at this moment but it's your future that counts from here on out, Wink, not the past. And you have so many good choices now."

Toni Canon knew her words sounded terribly lame but she couldn't resist any longer as she reached across the table to hold Wink's hand. "I'll help you anyway I can, I hope you know that."

Chapter 44

Deputy Canon spent several hours discussing her new found information about Wink Martin with the sheriff. She and her boss agreed that the information needed to be investigated completely with the Sausalito and San Francisco Police Departments and the sheriff assured her that it would be handled with the utmost discretion.

The facts regarding the robbery of his mother's art gallery, which Wink had described in detail, were unsubstantiated by the California authorities. The police department confirmed, however, that Gabriele Martin D'Angelo was deceased. He died as the result of serious bodily injuries received during an assault.

There had been an altercation at the gallery on the date in question which resulted in serious injuries to the owner and several other individuals, but no mention of robbery was ever included in the investigation. A police standoff between two rival gangs and the SF Police Dept. resulted in several more deaths near the art gallery including that of Leroy Jangles Carver, a major drug dealer from the West Coast. Carver's limo driver and a personal body guard also died at the scene. It had been an especially bloody weekend for law enforcement.

In the days following the incident, a severely beaten deceased body was found with papers that identified him as Gabriele Martin D'Angelo, the gallery owner's son, who was a seventeen-year-old male. Several grams of cocaine were located in the teen's clothing. The body had been identified and claimed shortly after the incident by the boy's grandmother, a prominent member of San Francisco society, Ms. Caroline Righetti. The young man was reportedly a former member of an affluent gang, The Streetsliders, which had been involved in several minor skirmishes with the law prior to the incident. According to law enforcement officials, the entire case was closed five years earlier.

Toni and the sheriff were actually relieved that their trusted friend did not have outstanding warrants in California. His amazing story would remain confidential until such time as Wink Martin – Gabriele Martin D'Angelo handled his status with the SF Police Department himself.

Chapter 45

Caroline Righetti was tending her flowers when the door-bell rang and her cousin, Angelina Robustelli informed her about the visitors. "La Polizia, Toni Canon." the heavy-set Italian woman said waving her hand toward the front door. Caroline put down her flower basket, clippers, and gloves and followed her gruff gray-haired cousin through the double French doors and into the living room. Soon after, her cousin Angelina disappeared once again to the back of the house.

Already incredibly nervous, Deputy Canon stood by the massive fireplace holding several of Chappy's personal pencil sketches along with the box containing the silk scarf when Caroline walked into the room. She expected that Ms. Righetti would be filled with bittersweet emotions after being informed of Charles Morgan's passing and her grandson's reappearance. Such information would be a lot for anyone to process and Toni wasn't quite sure what emotional reaction to anticipate from Wink's grandmother.

The young deputy felt a great sense of relief when the sheriff decided to personally notify Ms. Righetti about Gabriele's survival. Toni knew she was too close to Wink to be involved with Caroline at that level. She was extremely grateful for the sheriff's understanding.

Her boss was the ultimate professional and a sensitive family man. He knew Caroline Righetti needed time to deal with the emotional details of her grandson's situation. He had carefully explained the circumstances of Gabriele's disappearance by telephone in the days prior to the deputy's arrival in Monterey. The sheriff had given Caroline the gift of time....time to process the emotional reality of Chappy's death, Gabriele's life, as well as her personal grief regarding the misidentified young man presumed to be her grandson.

Toni suddenly felt awkward and out of her element. The silver-haired woman was simply stunning and Toni was struck by her breathtaking beauty immediately. She resembled a perfectly lovely porcelain doll. Caroline's soft dark eyes and quiet smile belied the extreme emotion hidden just below the surface, but she was an elegant lady who gracefully moved with relative ease across the large room to greet the deputy and Wink Martin. She was really very composed.

How could Morgan have left you Toni asked of herself silently as she reached out to shake Caroline's hand? You are so incredibly beautiful and kind. What was he thinking to run away to the old town of Stillwater and live like a hermit when you were here waiting for him all these years? All manner of questions raced through the deputy's mind as she observed Wink's grandmother in her own home. Toni Canon was deeply moved as she met Caroline Righetti for the first time.

The investigation was very personal to the young deputy and she was concerned with its uncertain outcome. She herself seemed more nervous than her hostess as she watched the beautiful woman from across the room. Toni adored her immediately and she cared deeply about Caroline's grandson.

As Toni Canon stood in the spectacular living room of 222 Sea Mist Drive, she was aflutter with emotions. She was treading on foreign ground as she realized she truly wanted a future with Gabriele D'Angelo regardless of his past.

Her emotions were suddenly crystal clear.

Wink stepped forward to help his grandmother sit down on a nearby sofa as she unexpectedly appeared faint at the sight of him, nearly losing her balance in the process. Toni Canon suddenly felt several tears roll gently down her cheeks as she watched Wink from across the room.

He knelt down in front of his grandmother with tears in his eyes as the elegant woman began to cry quietly. Touching his face tenderly with one hand and holding his hand close to her heart with the other, the silver-haired lady spoke to her grandson with love and affection.

"Gabriele D'Angelo is it really you? I can't believe my eyes, you dear boy. We thought you were dead and lost to us forever after that horrible night. Let me look at you, you've grown so tall and you're as handsome as your grandfather Morgan. You have the same gentle smile as he and the same curly blond hair. I just can't believe it's really you after all these years. Praise God, Gabriele, my prayers have been answered."

"It's me, Grandmother. It's really me" Wink said as he laid his head in his grandmother's lap and wept like a little boy. "I'm so glad to finally see you again. I was too scared and ashamed to tell anyone where I was and I figured you and Mom were better off without me in your lives. I've done so many bad things and I can't begin to make up for them. Grandmother, please forgive me."

"Hush now boy, there's nothing to forgive. We're family, you and I, and there's nothing for us to do but love one another. More than enough time has already been wasted that we can never get back, but we can cherish one another for as long as we live. I love you, Gabriele; nothing you could ever do would change that, young man. Wipe your tears now and tell your old Grandmother where you've been and how you are and then we'll go see your poor mother."

Chapter 46

Toni Canon was emotionally drained after the incredibly touching scene she had witnessed between Caroline Righetti and her grandson. Although she felt like an intruder during their emotional reunion, the young deputy had begun to see Gabriele in a totally new light. He was an independently strong, handsome, and proud man as well as a loving and devoted grandson.

After she presented the elegant lady Caroline with the pencil sketches she and Wink had found in Chappy's home along with the beautiful hand-painted silk scarf, the look on Caroline's face would have melted the heart of the worst criminal known to man. Her face glowed with everlasting affection for the artist who had broken her heart.

The beautiful silver-haired woman stared at Chappy's simple pencil sketches for several moments in complete silence and then held them to her breast in an attitude of solemn prayer with her eyes gently closed.

Looking directly at the deputy, she whispered a quiet "thank you" to Toni which unexpectedly brought a lump back to the deputy's throat. Toni suddenly found herself fighting back tears of her own once again.

It was a heart wrenching scene and one that Toni could not quite reconcile as she recollected the detestable way Charles Morgan abandoned the very people who loved him most. There were so many unanswered questions regarding the deceased professor, but Toni would have to leave them for another day.

A calm and sincere smile graced the kind woman's face as she opened the roughly carved wooden box and once again touched her very own hand-painted silk scarf she had worn so many years earlier. As she slowly lifted the scarf to her face she caressed its softness and remembered the long lost joy it had once given her. Caroline gently kissed the long flowing scarf and then effortlessly wrapped it around her hair just as she had done nearly fifty years earlier in the red and white Corvette convertible. The years melted away for a moment as Caroline once again became that lovely young woman whose life was filled with promise, hope, and so much love for the man of her dreams.

Chapter 47

The short drive into San Francisco took less than an hour. Toni was grateful for her GPS navigational system which guided her through the unfamiliar city directly to the correct address without any complications. Their destination, in the heart of the city, was the Winston family's mausoleum. As she and Wink helped Caroline out of the vehicle, a look of sadness swept across the older woman's face. In that instant Toni suddenly realized that Ivy Righetti D'Angelo was deceased.

Wink nodded to the young deputy in acknowledgement of her discovery without ever speaking a word. The two of them had simultaneously come to exactly the same conclusion and it was an intensely intimate and private moment for them to share. Toni looked into Wink's eyes for a long moment and felt a slow warmth building inside which caught her totally off-guard once again. She blushed crimson and quickly turned away to avoid Wink's detection.

Once again Toni thought of her beloved brother Andrew as the gold heart-shaped locked moved on its chain. She felt so many familiar feelings when she was with Wink Martin. It was confusing, as if she were sharing Andrew again. Was Gabriele D'Angelo her soul mate? Was her brother sending her a message?

As Wink and Toni held his grandmother's arms, the trio slowly walked toward the mausoleum. Caroline began to tell her version of the night that Gabriele Martin D'Angelo disappeared from San Francisco.

"I was never certain of exactly how it all happened, of course, only that your mother, my dear sweet Ivy had once again gotten herself involved with the wrong kind of man. She had a penchant for doing that and I've never been able to quite understand why."

"There was some sort of scuffle at her art show I believe. Ivy was with a huge burly black man who suddenly became maniacal after some rival drug dealers threatened him. Apparently he and several of his body guards beat poor Ivy without mercy and left her for dead in the alley behind her art gallery. She was such a gifted artist if only that had been enough for her. But, sadly it was not. She lost her life without every really understanding how to live. She was always a lost and lonely poor soul, when she had all that really mattered already within her easy reach. You were more than enough for her to love. I'm so sorry she let you down and herself as well. She could have had such a wonderful and happy life in this beautiful city with you and me and her amazing talents."

"Forgive me please, Deputy, I get carried away," Caroline said as she wiped her nose with a hankie.

"Now, where was I? Oh yes, she was badly beaten and barely alive when the police found her. She was taken to the hospital and they did all they could for her, but she had lain there alone for too long in the cold without treatment and her brain was severely damaged. She lived nearly six months hooked up to all sorts of tubes and machinery until finally her heart just gave out. It was a blessing really. She would never have wanted to exist like that. She was much too vain and too concerned with what other people thought. There was no hope for her recovery."

"The police called me about you, Gabriele, the very next day or two. They said your wallet and your personalized high school jacket had been found on a badly beaten body. I was out of my mind with heartbreak at the thought of losing both you and your mother. I went to the morgue to view the body.

But God knows that I could never really look at such a thing. I closed my eyes, prayed, and said it was you, dear boy. But praise God it was not. I've always kept a light on for you, Gabriele, hoping in my heart of hearts that I was wrong and that one fine day you would return. And now by the Grace of God, here you are."

"The poor young soul who lies in the vault next to your mother bears your name and must be given a new burial plot away from our family. What a sad thing that his own family has not missed him or searched for him. Oh dear, I claimed the wrong child. We must notify the police at once to set the record straight."

"We can take care of that soon, Ms. Righetti," Toni added reassuringly. "You certainly don't need to worry about that today."

"Thank you Toni, it is so nice to have you here with us." Caroline then added with a sly smile: "I can certainly see why Gabriele is so fond of you."

"Well now, Gabriele, it seems that the men responsible for your Mother's death were killed by the police in a dramatic gangland shoot out a day later so there's nothing more to be done about any of it. Ivy chose her own path even though it seemed sad and lonely to us and Lord knows I tried to show her a better way to live. She was hard-headed and strong willed just like her Grandfather Fredrick Winston, and there was just no taming her. I will forever miss her sweet smile and those cobalt blue eyes and that unruly red hair, just as I have missed your Grandfather Morgan for all these many years. But Ivy lived her life on her own terms just as Chappy did and that is all any of us can ask for isn't it?"

Wink was overcome with guilt and emotion as his grandmother spelled out the details of his mother's demise. Panic rose up in his voice as he gently spoke to the silver-haired matriarch he so revered.

"Let's sit down here a minute, Grandmother; there are some things I have to tell you before we go inside. I think it would be easier for you if you sit down for a few minutes."

Wink, Toni, and the elegant Caroline Righetti sat together on a marble bench just outside the mausoleum. They were surrounded by a collection of birds chirping joyously near a bubbling water fountain. The emotional day was bathed in bright sunshine. As they gazed across the cityscape they could see the Golden Gate Bridge off in the distance and Caroline spoke calmly about the wonderfully peaceful view.

"I'll be glad knowing there's such a beautiful view here when it's my turn to leave this world. I always thought I'd be here with my dear Charles someday and that Ivy would join us much, much later. Perhaps we can have him brought here after all Ms. Canon, will that be possible?"

"I'm sure it will be Ms. Righetti. I can see to the details personally as soon as I get back."

"Thank you, dear. That means a great deal to me. Please call me Caroline;" the silver-haired beauty added. "I can see that we are all good friends." Caroline shared an affectionate glance with her grandson and Toni Canon and patted each one gently on the knee. She could see for herself that there was more between the two young people than met the eye, so to speak. Caroline recognized the simple gaze that passed between her grandson and the young deputy as the look of abiding love she herself had known so well. She had seen the very same look on Chappy's face nearly fifty years earlier.

Wink could not hold back his words any longer as he blurted out with emotion: "Grandmother, I want you to know some things about the night my Mother was beaten. There are things that I should have told you long ago but I was too afraid to tell anyone, including the police. Instead I ran like a coward. It's my fault that Mom was killed, I should have gone to prison...."

Interrupting Wink as he tried to speak, his grandmother placed her finger upon his lips and wiped a tear from his face. "Hush now dear boy, I'll not hear another word of it. I might be old but I'm no fool. I have been around this earth for a good long while and I have always known there was more unhappiness attached to that terrible ugly story. But there's no need to share it now. It is long gone and finished so I don't want you to speak of it again. I was so afraid that you had come to the same terrible end as your mother on that horrible night, and I would have been unable to forgive myself if that had finally proved to be true. You are safe and sound, Gabriele, and that is all that matters to me now."

"You have a long and happy life ahead of you and I can see that you are off to a fine start with no thanks at all to your mother and father, and with very little help from me, I'm sorry to say. I am terribly ashamed to admit that I should have done more to intervene on your behalf. I simply could not find the strength to stand against your incredibly stubborn and defiant mother. I am afraid I spoiled her even as an adult and gave in far too often to her strong will and outlandish lifestyle. Her personality was never suited for such privilege and wealth and I should have restricted her frivolous access to so much money. But sadly I did not and now it is I who must ask for your forgiveness and understanding."

"Please don't talk like that, Grandmother. There's nothing for me to forgive and I truly understand completely. You could not have changed what happened. Mom made all of her own choices. She knew how to behave much better at the time and she still made the same bad decisions. No one could change her choices; she needed to do that for herself but she wasn't strong enough. I love you Grandmother and I am grateful I still have the chance to get to know you and to spend some time with you."

"I can see for myself that you are a good strong man, Gabriele. I am proud to have you as my one and only grandson. You have already survived more heartache and difficulty than most people experience in a lifetime, and I know you will do your very best to be the kind of man you were always meant to become. You have the world at your finger-tips, my boy, and I believe you will leave it in much better condition than you found it. Let's go in now and have a short visit with your mother and some other members of our family. This is certainly no place for the living."

Chapter 48

The investigation of Charles Morgan's property was frustrating for the Churchill County Sheriff's Department or (CCSD). The sheriff did not find the immediate results he hoped for and a sense of desperation and disappointment washed over him. The sheer size of the acreage in question made any further detailed exploration cost-prohibitive for his small police department. With the economy at an all-time low, the budget for his office had been greatly reduced.

The sheriff had been so certain there were countless secrets to be discovered near the old man's home but it was beginning to look like he was totally incorrect. He'd even gone out on a limb and wagered a bet with one of his deputies. He knew better than to proceed on a hunch, but this one seemed to have bested him.

The pieces of hard evidence the sheriff relied on were the clean skull Deputy Canon located in the root cellar and the few unusual personal drawings found among Morgan's possessions. And even that was fairly speculative one must admit.

Privately the sheriff acknowledged to himself that he might have jumped to conclusions about Charles Morgan. His job as the chief lawman had become rather monotonous over the course of a few years and the mysterious Chappy Morgan presented a challenge he gladly welcomed. Had this law enforcement official let his imagination run away with him to the exclusion of common sense – or was there actually something to his notion about the old professor?

It was entirely plausible the reclusive old man had stumbled upon the skull at some point in his travels and decided to keep the relic for his own fascination. It was circumstantial evidence at best without proof that a crime had even been committed. A similar judgment could be made regarding the black and orange California license plate found on a birdhouse in the old man's yard as well as the pencil sketch that was located in his collection of notebooks. The license plate may have been something the old codger found on his journeys to Stillwater Point Reservoir and had nothing whatsoever to do with criminal activity. After all, Charles Preston Morgan was an eccentric old man long before his death.

The large cache of money found in the underground storage room legitimately belonged to Morgan as the bank in San Francisco had proved by notarized documentation. There was no secret hidden there. It merely provided honest evidence of the old man's great success as an educator and business man.

Although the CCSD contracted with the forensic departments of several agencies for ground penetrating radar and excavating experts, their limited searches produced few results. The first successful find was of a buried vehicle which befuddled the sheriff strictly because of its location. The truck, or what little there was left of it after more than forty years beneath the alkaline soil with a high water table, was presumed to be a classic old El Camino Chevrolet. But that was just a best-guess by the forensic technicians on site. Years underground had taken its toll on the old artifact and all the earth yielded to the sheriff was a rusted and crumbling metal skeleton.

There was no paint left on the vehicle remains.

There was no chrome and not a single tire had survived the pitch black grave. The rusty thing was rotted to pieces, crumbling apart, and that's all there was to it. A connection to the pencil sketch of the El Camino that Chappy drew was difficult to define although the sheriff found the etched words: *end of the road* to be quite haunting. The vehicle's license plates were rusted away to nearly nothing and that was also disappointing.

The bolts were still visible where they were originally attached to the car frame, but there were no distinguishing marks left behind. The badly corroded license plates were barely attached to the crumbling truck body. That fact totally eliminated a possible connection to the California plate #5KGQ436 the sheriff carried in his vest pocket. In spite of his persistence and best efforts there was no evidence to match to the El Camino and he was a bit angry with the situation.

The sheriff felt a wave of disappointment wash over him once again. He wanted better definitive answers for young Wink Martin but it looked like none of the puzzle pieces were falling easily into place about Chappy Morgan.

The professor's junk yard was filled with automobile skeletons left in plain view — why then had Morgan buried this particular El Camino he wondered? And had the old man really buried the car himself? Perhaps the previous property owner who developed the junk yard had actually been the one to bury the vehicle? Stranger things had been done and there was no way to know for certain. After all, there was a '57 Chevy in plain sight along with a '68 Thunderbird not fifty yards away. Both cars had been completely destroyed by fire and rust so why weren't they hidden away in the junkyard or buried like the El Camino?

The sheriff was even less certain a crime had been committed after the technicians found no evidence inside the rusted-out El Camino and no indication the owner's body had been present at the time of burial. The sheriff was overcome with doubt.

Could the El Camino possibly belong to the Aisan man whose skull was discovered in Chappy's root cellar? It was doubtful the Chevrolet could be identified by its deteriorated VIN number, but only time would tell after the old records were located. The sheriff wanted some answers before Wink Martin returned from Monterey, but Chappy Morgan seemed to be keeping him off his game.

The old outhouse was finally demolished and the remains were removed by a county bulldozer. The sheriff held onto some hope that evidence of criminal activity would still be found as the old pit toilet was thoroughly searched by experts. His rejection intensified when there was nothing of consequence found.

The countless bags of lye used to sanitize the deep pit toilet over the years completely destroyed any evidence that may have been dumped there. If anything or anyone had had been thrown inside, it was likely all trace evidence was eaten by the caustic chemical. Forty years is a long time for any evidence to survive especially in such rustic and primitive conditions. Soft alkali dirt and some very small broken pieces of glass were all that was recovered when the technicians finished their search.

The sheriff and his crew noticed rather quickly, however, that the area became very quiet and peaceful without the outhouse door swaying in the breeze. The unusual silence drew everyone's attention. Without the crusty hinges howling up a storm, a man could actually hear himself think.

"Do you believe in ghosts?" the sheriff asked a technician as they were packing their gear.

"No, Sir, I can't say that I do. But this is certainly the kind of place I'd look for them if ever I was so inclined. There's a feeling I get out here that I've never felt anywhere else – a type of heavy solitude filled with a sensation of intense spirits."

"It feels kind of spooky to me actually. Guess that's why I shy away from thoughts and activities of the occult. Just being out here gives me the creeps and that's something I've never admitted to anyone before. I feel death on this property, Sir, and it scares me something awful. As a kid, my folks used to tell me that ghosts are souls trapped between heaven and earth. As spirits, the souls are terribly restless and unhappy and they have to spend eternity trying to get home. I wouldn't wish that fate for anyone."

"That's an intriguing idea, Son. I think your parents may be correct. I feel pretty much the same way. But there's one more thing that I feel for certain about this property and it's all about secrets. Morgan kept a lot of secrets. I think there are many of them hidden here on this property that may never be discovered unless someone really digs through this old man's life. His secrets could provide the portal these ghosts need to find their way home."

On the drive back into town, the sheriff paused to reflect on his opinions of Charles Morgan. Perhaps the old man was truly a salt-of-the-earth guy who lived alone, drew pictures of birds and insects, and minded his own business for forty-four years. And maybe, just maybe, that wasn't the whole truth about the old codger at all. The sheriff was certain Chappy's rocking chair could provide the pivotal piece of evidence to prove his theory one way or the other. The belt inscribed with Jangles' name was real and tangible. The sheriff had seen it and touched it for himself.

According to the California authorities, Leroy Carver, the man who called himself Jangles, had died in San Francisco a few years earlier. He had been involved with Chappy's daughter Ivy Marie D'Angelo. And one thing was certain: the Morgan family dynamics had proved to be very complicated and convoluted. The sheriff was unclear exactly how involved the reclusive Morgan truly was with his own family or how much he had known about his former lover and her daughter and grandson. It was certainly possible that he knew nothing. Not the usual scenario at all, but still possible.

Although Leroy Carver's father, Wilson, had been missing for about forty years, the sheriff knew he was a reputed drug lord also known as Jangles Carver. One of the two men, father or son, intentionally or by accident left the leather belt behind with Chappy Morgan. That was not a coincidence.

Instinctively the sheriff concluded that action came with a very high price tag attached. With a little common sense and some deductive reasoning, he believed the belt's owner to be the missing father, Wilson Carver. The age and wear of the belt seemed to fit that scenario. But how could he prove it without a body or any kind of real proof? It was amazing to the sheriff that such a possible and serious crime could be forty years old and remain completely undetected. It was all about the secrets.

Caroline Righetti appeared to be the only living link that could possibly connect all of the missing pieces and people together. Perhaps she had information that she was not even consciously aware of. The sheriff made a mental note to spend some time with her in the near future. He could always justify a trip into the city for work related issues. He had a long list of questions for the elegant lady and he hoped she could provide him with some quick accurate answers. Time was of the essence.

One day the lawman intended to learn the truth about the eccentric old man who spent forty-four years in Stillwater, Nevada protecting his secrets. He couldn't explain his feelings. He just felt deep in his gut that there was much more to Chappy Morgan than anyone knew. Call it a lawman's hunch.

Charles Preston Morgan was a ghost in his own life.....and the sheriff was determined to know why.

The End

www.ingramcontent.com/pod-product-compliance
Lightning Source LLC
Chambersburg PA
CBHW051514170626
46811CB00002B/821